The Fall
of
Heaven
Hill

The Fall of Heaven Hill

Charles Martinez

THE FALL OF HEAVEN HILL

iUniverse books may be ordered through booksellers or by contacting:

iUniverse
1663 Liberty Drive
Bloomington, IN 47403
www.iuniverse.com
1-800-Authors (1-800-288-4677)

ISBN: 978-1-5320-8128-6 (sc)
ISBN: 978-1-5320-8129-3 (e)

Print information available on the last page.

iUniverse rev. date: 01/14/2020

A small token in memory
of a place and a way of life in another time.

For my wife, Esther,
and for my parents, Adelina and Mandy.

There is nothing left of the high old town in the mountains of southeastern Arizona. Hill by hill it slowly disappeared into thin air. Those hills had names and houses and people. There may come a day when the call of handed-down stories draws people up into those mountains in search of a trace of what once was. They will find only a high and airy emptiness. Then they will wonder if the town ever really existed.

1

In the early years of Sal's long military career, he and Ben wrote back and forth but as time went on the letters dwindled down until they eventually came to an end. People change. People move apart and move on. It was just one of those things.

The old mining town of Orenville held little attraction for Sal. His last visit had been in the bitter-cold winds of February in 1976. During the years of his absence he had forgotten about those winds and how the ground became bare and cracked and frozen. The dust and grit and occasional snowflake swirled down into his mother's open grave. It seemed to Sal that the wind blew nonstop for three days.

Sal had seen much of the world during his career. He had been to Paris and Rome and the Vatican and the Coliseum and Jerusalem and the Nile and the pyramids of Egypt. He had seen Big Ben and Buckingham Palace and the bullfights in Pamplona on July afternoons. He could tell first- hand stories about all those places in addition to many others. Master Sergeant Sal Madrid was a worldly man.

After Sal retired from the Army and after his final trip into Mexico (the tour bus company he was driving for was bought out by another company) he resolved to get back in touch with his old friend and *compadre*. A stranger's voice answered Ben's old telephone number in Orenville. The lady told him Ben had moved away. The lady, whose name sounded familiar to Sal although he

1

could not recall exactly who she was, told him Ben had moved to California to live with his daughter, Sara, who was also Sal's goddaughter. The woman wasn't sure about anything else except to say he might call a friend of Sara's and gave him her number. Sal called the young lady who told him she had not heard from Sara for some time but that she did have her last address.

A week later Sal was on the plane to San Francisco where he rented a car and drove down to San Jose. He located the house, but a Vietnamese family was living there. The kindly woman at the door told him in broken English that they had been there for two years and didn't know who lived there before them. Sal thanked her and walked away.

The trip had been a long shot to start with. A dead end meant the search was over and that meant he would probably never see Ben again. The realization hit home as Sal sat in the car and wondered at all the years gone by. Old memories sprang up as he drove back to the freeway and headed north to San Francisco. The clear view of the sparkling bay and green hills and blue sky brought back the image of a similar day when he and Ben came up that same highway on a Greyhound bus. They came to see the city for the first time from basic training at Fort Ord. Two young soldiers on a weekend pass with everything in front of them. The memory of that brilliant day grew and seemed far and near at the same time. The past and the present. The number of years in between seemed impossible to Sal.

After a few days in the city Sal decided to stay. He rented a furnished apartment close to Golden Gate Park and settled in.

One morning a short time later Sal walked out of a restaurant on the corner of Cole and Haight streets and bumped into Phil Esterly, an old classmate from Orenville. They spoke for a while about high school and the old town and then Sal asked if by any chance Phil might know anything about Ben Medina. Phil told Sal that he himself didn't keep up with things back home but that his younger brother, Lee, did.

That night Lee called Sal. Lee's family had moved to Orenville from Oklahoma during the boom times of the mid-forties and early fifties when the mine expanded greatly. At that time the new housing in the Anglo section on the other side of one of the hills of the old town had not yet been completed, so it was that a few of the new arrivals including the Lesterlys rented houses on Heaven Hill until those new houses were finished. Sal recalled that after the move Lee used to come back and visit friends up on Heaven Hill and also that Lee spoke excellent Spanish due to the fact that he'd had a Mexican nanny during his grade school years.

Lee was a professor of economics at San Francisco State College. He told Sal that a few years prior he and a couple of his colleagues had received a grant for the purpose of researching the history of labor in the copper industry in the Southwest. He said that the most difficult company to obtain any historical information from was the Dome Corporation. According to Lee, "*Todo es un secreto para esa compania.*"

In the course of the conversation, Lee mentioned that he'd been publishing a monthly newsletter about Orenville for some time. Occasionally, he would publish obituaries. Sal was surprised at the number of schoolmates who'd passed on.

Lee said he hadn't heard anything from or about Ben for several years except for a vague rumor that he'd been involved in some kind of incident with the company. And then nothing else until two years before when he received a letter from Ben with a check for seven hundred dollars. Lee said this was enough money to finance the newsletter for quite some time. He gave Sal Ben's address, which sounded to Sal like some old folk's home in Scottsdale, Arizona.

As they were about to hang up Lee said, "You know, Sal, there comes a time to call a spade a spade. No way around it. The truth of the matter is that those secretive sons of bitches had their own little fiefdom going on up there. Pure and simple. We, the kids, all of us, no matter what we looked like, be it white, brown, red, or black did not create that society. We had no hand in it. We were born into it or brought into it and then we were locked into it. We sat side by side in school and we had friends, good friends, among the different groups and we played and teased and laughed and fought and had infatuations between us but when the bell rang after school some of us went home in one direction and some of us in another. That's just the way it was. Now, old friend, I have searched high and low for the proper academic term to describe that nonsense, but I finally gave up and settled on just calling it a truckload of hand-picked, high-grade horseshit."

Sal laughed. "It was what it was, Lee."

"Yeah, I know, Sal. But still...."

A few days later Sal walked into the tastefully furnished lobby of the Rose Garden. A tall, attractive woman came out of the door of the office behind the counter.

"Good morning, sir. May I help you?"

"Yes, good morning, my name is Sal Madrid. I am here to see Ben Medina." Sal smiled at the woman.

The woman smiled back. "Let me see if I can locate him, Mr. Madrid. Please have a seat."

Sal sat in one of the plush chairs and picked up a glossy brochure from a small table on which there was a vase with fresh red roses. The cover of the brochure read: "Welcome to the Best Retirement Community in the Valley."

Sal looked at the advertisement with interest since the cover had a picture of an attractive lady decked out in a tennis outfit. The lady in the picture very much resembled the lady at the counter who was now speaking into the telephone. According to the brochure, the Rose Garden had much to offer including housekeeping and nurses on duty and a visiting physician and aides who made sure the residents maintained any prescribed medical regimen. It had a spa and a heated swimming pool and a state-of-the-art exercise facility. The two-story apartment complex curved around spacious grounds as shown in a foldout map and behind the complex there was a walking trail that wound its way through a large orange tree orchard. On the other side of the orchard there was another smaller complex designated as the "Assisted Living" Rose Garden. As Sal waited and glanced about, he saw several silver-haired people strolling by. Then, looking down the hallway, Sal saw a heavy-set man limping toward the lobby. Not wanting to stare, Sal looked away but after a few moments he was compelled to look back at the man who was now crossing the lobby.

Sal was stunned. The man who approached him was Ben, but a Ben heavier by fifty pounds or more since the last time Sal had seen him. As they embraced, and not sure just exactly what to say, Sal said, "Benny Boy, what the hell are you doing living here with all these relics?"

Ben didn't answer Sal's question. Instead, he said, *"Cuantos años son, Salvador?"* Sal hadn't known what to answer, not because he wasn't sure of the number of years since they had last seen each other, but because he had no response for the reproach in Ben's voice.

As Ben led Sal away back down the hallway and out into the courtyard, Sal asked, "Why the limp, Ben?"

Ben did not look at Sal but looked straight ahead and said, in the same tone as before, "If a guy would stay in touch, he might know."

Back in Ben's apartment, he called down to the dining hall and ordered roast beef sandwiches for lunch. The sandwiches were delivered on a large silver platter along with French fries and deep-fried onion rings. They had cold beer with their food. The conversation went along in bits and pieces—the news, the weather. Sal knew that Ben was hurt with him. Too many years had gone by for being out of touch between two old friends. But what Sal also knew was that it had been Ben himself who had stopped writing. It seemed to Sal that Ben had forgotten that part of it. But now, thought Sal, was not the time to get into that business. Sal decided to take the lead, and the blame. "Ben, I'm sorry I didn't stay in touch all these years."

Ben stopped eating and looked away, out of the window to the trees in the courtyard. He looked back at Sal and with a softer voice said, "That's okay, Sal."

"You have a nice place here, Ben."

"Yes, well, they take good care of us."

"The people here, are they okay with you?"

"Yes, I have friends."

Sal laughed. "But they're all old, right?"

"Old? Did you say old?" Ben's face turned red. "*I* am old, Sal. I don't know about you."

Sal was on the verge of clarifying his words but at that moment two attractive women happened to walk by Ben's living room window. Sal heard the pleasing sound of their laughter. He sat up and said, "Hold the phone." Ben smiled for the first time.

After lunch, Sal stepped into the bathroom for a minute and when he came back out Ben was already asleep in his recliner. He was breathing deeply with his head back and to one side with his mouth slightly open. Sal sat down and looked at his old friend. The buttons on Ben's shirt were stretched out tightly, as though they could pop out at any minute. Sal looked at Ben in disbelief.

Ben had changed, Sal knew. It wasn't merely the weight gain; something inside had changed as well. Sal sat silent and thought about what he should do. The Rose Garden seemed very nice and comfortable and secure and it could well be the best in the valley as advertised, but to Sal the idea of living in a retirement community was simply out of the question. He thought he could just leave a note and be gone. Then, he saw in the now relaxed features a hint of the old Ben and realized he couldn't leave. "Ben?" Sal spoke in a voice slightly louder than normal conversation. Ben opened his eyes. "What?"

"I read in that brochure down in the lobby that you have a walking trail back there somewhere."

"What about it?" There was irritation in Ben's voice.

"Well, why don't you and I go down there and check it out?"

Ben did not respond. Instead, he closed his eyes again.

"Well, what do you say, Ben?"

Surprisingly agile in spite of the weight gain, Ben jumped to his feet. His face was flushed. "What are you trying to say? That I am overweight? Go ahead and say it, you…" Ben advanced a step toward Sal.

Sal looked away for a moment. In his long career he had dealt with hard-nosed soldiers of every shape, size, and attitude and had at his disposal any number of equally hard responses for such occasions. But now he looked up at the face of his old friend and spoke with a measured voice. "Come on, Ben. No one said anything about that."

Ben stared at Sal, his mouth open and working, trying to get the words out. Sal met his stare for a moment and then turned away. He shook his head slowly and spoke softly. "*No la chinges, mano. Que bárbaro.*"

Ben sat back down. The anger passed as quickly as it had risen. The stern look on his face was gone, replaced by a hint of unease or discomfort.

Sal smiled at Ben until he got a small smile back. He waited a moment longer and then said, "So, old codger pal of mine, now that you mention it, why don't we go down there and walk off a French fry or two?"

Ben laughed in spite of himself.

The walking trail was a long winding pathway through and around the large orange tree orchard. Ben complained often but when he was not complaining he and Sal spoke of old times and home. As they spoke, Sal saw glimpses of the old Ben but slightly different somehow. Something elusive. Almost as though a part of him had worn away or become dormant.

A week later Sal acquired the lease to the apartment directly below Ben's.

"Are you sure about this, Sal?"

"Nope, not sure at all, man. The thing is I used to know a guy who kind of reminds me of you." Sal looked at Ben, studying him. "Although he was better looking and about half your size." Sal held up his hand in a gesture to keep Ben from speaking up. "So, someone needs to stick around here and see if there's something to be done about that. Yes sir, someone definitely needs to look into that."

2

Ben comes slowly out of his dream into the pale glow of dawn. For a moment the images of his dream hold. He had climbed Heaven Hill by moonlight to stand in the ruins of the old mill. There were footprints in the dust by a long row of pillars of old concrete. A young woman in a blue velvet dress called to him from the shadows. She called him by another name….

Ben remains still, waiting for the first hint of pain in his right leg. There are days when the discomfort is bearable, and it is at those times when he is not sure if the pain is in his leg or in his head. There are other times when there is no question. Today, there is no pain.

Ben moans anyway, out of habit. He tucks his hands behind his head and looks up at the ceiling where the faint morning light has made the ceiling the color of a golden rose, or maybe a peach. He closes his eyes and listens for the familiar whir of the elevator and the sound of footsteps on the walkway by his second story apartment. Ben closes his eyes tighter. *The shadows were blue in the moonlight; the pillars were bone white.*

A moment later there is the sound of his front door opening and the click of the light switch. Sal's voice calls out, loud and cheerful. "Rise and shine, Benny Boy. The coffee's getting cold and you're getting old. Be bold, man. Make a statement. Get up for God's sake."

Ben turns his head slowly to look at Sal, who as usual is sharply dressed. He is wearing a light-gray pullover sweater over a white shirt and slacks of a darker shade of gray and shiny black loafers of woven leather. Sal is very fit. At most, he may have gained five or ten pounds since high school. He has thick, wavy, silver hair and a gold tooth. It is not the whole front tooth but rather the tooth is outlined in gold.

Sal looks down at Ben and shakes his head. He begins to move in a slow circle at the foot of the bed, shadowboxing. Sal matches his words to the rhythm of his footwork.

"Jab…right cross…uppercut. Take that, and that, and that. I will teach you a lesson, Mad Dog, and your face is the blackboard."

"What time is it, Sal?" Ben asks, not moving from his bed. There had been something familiar about the young woman's smile.

"Half past time to get up, man." Sal has now decked his imaginary opponent and begins to count. "One…two…ten… you're out!" In another voice he says, "Hold on there, ref. You didn't give my boy the full count." A worried frown appears on Sal's face as he moves on to the next line. "Sarge, I strongly suggest you get your boy back to his corner before they arrest me and you both as accomplices to manslaughter."

The scene is from a story Ben told Sal about his boxing career in the Army. Sal has rearranged and embellished it.

"That's not the way it went Sal, but I'm glad I've got you around to tell me what happened in my own life."

"Damn right."

Ben yawns and turns away. A thought crosses his mind, again. It is the idea that in some hole-in-the-wall store somewhere in the Southside, Sal has found the bottled water of the Fountain of Youth. He imagines Sal coming out of that tiny store with a great big blue plastic jug slung up over his shoulder. On Ben's good days it is a thought that gives him the pleasure of indignation. It is much the same feeling he has when he hears some of Sal's fantastic stories about his travels in Mexico, usually dealing with the amazing powers of plants and herbs whose names sound entirely made up to Ben. The names always seem to have a double meaning. The trouble is that Ben doesn't think about the second meaning until Sal is gone. Sal calls those times his "days of wine and Rositas."

Sal comes around the bed. He looks down into Ben's face. "You *are* getting up today, right, Combs?" The name sounds like *combs*. Ben thinks it might be Sal's personal rendition of *compa* which is short for *compadre*, but with Sal it could be something else altogether. It could be a combination of *compa* and *homes*. Sometimes it sounds like *cones*, which might be short for *concuño* and means co-brother-in-law. (Their wives, gone many years, were sisters.) Ben thinks maybe someday he will ask Sal about it, and then again maybe he won't.

Ben sighs and sits up. The memory of his dream glimmers briefly in his mind and floats away.

Sal turns on the television set while Ben goes into the bathroom to wash up and shave. Ben can hear Sal talking to the female news commentator through the open bathroom door, but his words are drowned out by the sound of the electric shaver. Ben brushes his teeth and then puts a small amount of toothpaste into his left hand. He looks down at his hand for a moment and laughs at himself while he rinses the toothpaste off. He takes some after-shave lotion, dilutes it with water, and rubs it vigorously into his face. Ben combs his sometimes-unruly salt-and-pepper hair straight back and then closes the door. He sits on the edge of the bathtub and recites three prayers. He takes his time.

When Ben comes back out of the bathroom, he sees that Sal has already laid out his clothes for him. Overlapping slightly on the bed are a pair of tan slacks, a white shirt, and a dark green pullover sweater. Sal insists on going with Ben when it is time to buy clothes. Ben shakes his head and makes a move toward the closet but Sal steps in front of him.

"What? You're not going to shower today?"

"I showered during the night, Sal." Sometimes at night when Ben can't sleep, he gets up and takes a cold or hot shower depending on the season.

"I thought I heard the shower last night." Sal waits a moment. "So, did you have the Countess in there with you?"

The person Sal is referring to is Helen Petrovich. Ben thinks it is because Helen is Russian that Sal calls her the Countess. Ben has never asked Sal for an explanation. He has never asked because he suspects that somewhere in Sal's response there will be a punch line.

Ben doesn't answer Sal's question as he finishes dressing and then he and Sal walk out of the door. They ride down the elevator and across the dewy grass of the perfectly manicured lawn of the Rose Garden to the dining hall. The early dawn air is quite cool, as though autumn is on the way. The reflection of the light on the white eaves of the dining hall and the smell of the coffee remind Ben of another time, another life. A flash of a memory moves through his mind, an image of coming home in the fall along the road above his house and seeing the light from his kitchen window through the branches of the cottonwood trees in his front yard. There were two trees, male and female. One was slender and tall, and the other was thicker and taller. Ben remembers the turning of the leaves to gold in the fall. Later, the snow would come.

Words form in Ben's mind. *The weather turned warm and then it snowed.* A second memory follows of a cold, star-filled night in winter when he'd gone to return a book to a friend on another hill. Walking back to his house along the well-worn footpath, Ben took off his jacket as the weather seemed to change and turn mild, even warm in comparison. The stars lit his way. He paused in his yard and looked up through the bare branches of the trees at the heavens in pleasant weather. The following morning the town was covered in a blanket of snow and it was still falling.

Inside the dining hall there is the murmur of much conversation. As Ben and Sal walk toward the back of the dining hall, Ben waves at Helen. She smiles at him and waves back. Sal makes a sound in his throat. "Yessiree, looks like she showered during the night, too." Ben pretends he doesn't hear Sal's comment. Sal walks away to talk to a few of his lady friends and some of the men along the way and then joins Ben at their regular table.

"You remember old Healy, right?" Sal says.

"John Healy?"

"Yeah, him. Bit the dust. Bill Jones wants to have a little get-together with you and me and Hank and Ross in his honor tonight."

As these words are being spoken, Patience Taylor, the directress of the Rose Garden, comes walking by the long row of windows of the dining hall. She is a tall, friendly, attractive woman and her appearance in the dining hall at breakfast time usually means that someone has died or been transferred to the assisted living facility of the Rose Garden. As soon as she enters the dining hall the chattering begins to die down.

"Please, ladies and gentlemen." Patience stands by the piano in the corner of the dining hall. "I have an announcement." There is a moment of silence after the announcement about "our dear John" and then Patience says, "Claire? Would you be so kind?"

"Certainly," says Claire Chandler as she stands up. Ben has heard that Claire was a concert pianist in her youth. She is pretty and smiles easily and her white hair is always perfectly done, and it reminds Ben of the soft white clouds of summer. Claire arrives at the piano and sits down and then pauses for a few moments before she begins to play. An older man, a new resident who has not yet been introduced, throws his arms up in the air and exclaims loudly that he "can't hear a goddamned thing." No one pays him any mind. Finally, Claire begins playing "Amazing Grace" which she plays quite beautifully almost all the way through but then changes, somehow, into "The Star-Spangled Banner" and then on to a third song that Ben can't recognize at all.

3

A little past six in the evening Ben and Sal arrive at Bill's apartment for a poker party in honor of the departed. Ben had been to those kinds of parties before and did not want to go. He would have rather stayed in his own apartment and gotten some work done on his book. He agreed to go only after Sal's persistence wore him out. Walking in the door it was clear that the three men present had gotten a head start on the get together. Bill, Ross, and Hank have been friends with Ben since shortly after he moved into the Rose Garden. They are good men but at times they can be a bit crotchety and eccentric.

The men drink a toast of bourbon with beer chasers and buy their chips and light the expensive cigars Bill has provided for the occasion. It seems there has been an ongoing dispute between Ross and Hank about whether the departed was from Indiana or Illinois. It is important that Healy be from one place or the other. That argument is followed by another about whether John Healey's middle name was Hurley or Harley. This discussion goes on until both men rise to their feet.

"Gentlemen, gentlemen," Bill interrupts, "please; we're here to honor John. Come on now, we're all friends here. How about it, Sal, heard any good jokes lately?"

"You bet," Sal answers, and reels off three new jokes. Ben has no idea where Sal gets them from, maybe he invents them, but soon everyone is laughing loudly and mellowed out and having a good time.

After a couple of hands Bill sets out a large platter with summer sausage, cheese, crackers, and olives along with napkins and small decorative plates. While Ross is eating, he looks over at Sal and says, "By the way, Sal, I don't believe I've ever heard where you're from."

Before Sal can answer, Hank says, "He's from Orenville, same as Ben."

"He can answer for himself, Hank."

"Well, sure he can, but I'm telling you that he is from Orenville." The two men lock eyes, ready to rise again.

"That's right," Sal laughs. "The copper capital of the world."

Ross releases his stare and looks over at Sal. "I read an article about it here a while back. It said they had shut that place down." On his plate remains a single thin sesame seed cracker. He slides it around with his finger and then leaves it. "Company town, right?"

"That it was, my friend."

"The Dome Corporation?"

"Yes. Do you know that company?" Sal smiles.

"No, not really. But it's hard to believe that a company could own a whole town."

"Owned it lock, stock, and barrel, partner. You had to get permission to pee in your own toilet. Ben here is writing a book about it."

"Hard to believe, for sure." Ross picks up his cigar and puffs away trying to get it going again while across the table Bill moans as he studies his cards. He moans again and says some words no one understands.

Ross stares at him. "Say what?"

Hank laughs. "Tell the bartender to cut that man off right now."

Bill looks around, nervous and unsure. He sits up and clears his throat. "I said, does Ben own a book or did a company write about it." There is a brief silence and then laughter. Ben picks up his cards and arranges them. He wishes Sal wouldn't mention his

14

book. He is not sure what other people would call it although he himself has settled on the term "pictorial history." He has a box full of old photographs of Orenville and with them he intends to create a pictorial history of the town.

Ben's thoughts begin to drift to his collection as the conversation moves along to other matters. A picture of three people walking along the curve of a dirt road comes to his mind. The caption for it has been giving him trouble, and he thinks maybe he has hit upon the proper wording for it.

The sound of Bill's agitated voice draws him back to the table. "By God, I know my rights. This is my apartment and you can't throw me out." To which Ross and Hank say that they can damn sure throw him out as long as they can get enough votes to do so. There are some residents of the Rose Garden who are pretty high on voting. It's like a hobby for them and there is always some petition making the rounds. Ben has seen dozens. They turn in the petitions to Patience with no apparent result except when they have something to do with the menu.

As Bill opens a bottle of beer at Ben's side, a wisp of vapor rises from the mouth of the bottle and the smell of it suddenly carries him back to an event in his youth. He is home, and everything is very clear. He is wearing an old pair of shoes that are too tight because he had to save his good shoes for school. It is a certain Saturday in May. Dawn is breaking, and he is running to meet up with Sal and Danny Rios. His feet barely touch the hard-packed clay of the ground as he races along the road behind Heaven Hill.

"You in, Ben?" Sal asks.

Startled, Ben comes back and looks at Sal's face. In the previous second, in his mind, he had seen Sal as a young boy.

"No, Sal, I…I'm out. You can have my chips. I think I'm done for the night." Ben stands up and smiles.

"Are you okay, Ben?" Sal stands also as a worried look comes across his face. There had been something different in Ben's eyes.

"Yeah, sure. You guys go on. Just a little tired here. Goodnight, gentlemen."

The old memory returns as Ben makes his way back to his apartment by the dim lights under the rosebushes along the curving sidewalk. The images of that long-ago morning are clear as he passes by Helen's apartment where her curtains are open slightly and through which he catches a glimpse of her sitting on the couch by the flickering blue light of the television. Ben looks away and wonders at what might have been.

He pauses at his front door to check his mailbox as a thought slips by. Something about some other thing about a letter or words written on a piece of paper. Then it is gone. He walks in and goes straight to his bedroom where he brings down a metal box and accordion file from the top shelf of the closet and places them on the bed. He goes to the kitchen and pours himself a drink. He looks at the glass for a moment or two, then leaves it on the counter and goes to the bathroom. As he washes up and brushes his teeth, he tries to remember something that won't come. The feeling passes, and he walks out of the bathroom and gets into bed. He tapes two pictures onto a notebook of legal-size sheets of paper and begins to make notes by each picture. Using a magnifying glass, Ben studies the details of the old black-and-white photographs and is once again surprised at what magnification can reveal. There are things long missed and unnoticed in the background and shadows.

One of the old photographs brings to Ben's mind a later one in color. He goes through his collection and finds it. It is a winter morning and the town is covered in snow. The tall pines of the plaza and the three-story company store and the long flight of steps down to the high school are sharply etched into the soft whiteness. There is the deep-blue sky above Heaven Hill. Ben's eyes move along the familiar winding roads and trails he would run up each day from the high school to his house for lunch.

He selects another picture where three friends in caps and gowns smile by the steps of the church. Danny Rios stands in the middle with his arms around the shoulders of Ben and Sal. In the background other graduates are being photographed. Ben recognizes them all. He studies the picture until his eyes tire and begin to droop. He reaches over to turn off his bedside lamp and notices the paper cup the aide put out that morning still contains his pills. He is not sure what to do. After some thought he decides that if he has to get up during the night, he can take them then. Ben turns off the light and leans back against his pillow as thoughts and images of other pictures come into his mind down to the old photograph of a portion of the long and narrow road leading up to Orenville. The road climbed and curved seven miles up into the hills and canyons through light and shadow to reach and pass through a tunnel in the side of a mountain. Then it climbed higher still to reach the town. It was a town hard to get to, a place high and rugged and isolated and the only way out was back down that same road. Ben's last thought before drifting off is the image of himself standing far away, looking back. He can't see the town, only the winding road going up and disappearing into the hills.

4

S al leaves his apartment and walks through the orchard to the assisted living complex of the Rose Garden. He enters the office of Dr. Miles Birch and begins his usual banter and flirtation with Dahlia, the receptionist-assistant. Dahlia has a pretty face. She is middle aged and approaching plumpness.

She stands up and walks slowly to a filing cabinet where she pulls two folders. Sal watches her and does a low, soft whistle.

Dahlia chuckles and pretends to yawn. Sal's eyes light up. "Hold it right there, missy. I get the picture loud and clear. Time for bed. And in the middle of the day, no less."

"Shush, you. The doctor is waiting."

"And a good thing it is, little one." Sal winks and smiles. "Because, come on, who in his right mind could resist?"

Dahlia laughs out loud and waves him toward the doctor's door.

Dr. Birch stands and shakes Sal's hand as he walks in. Dr. Birch is in his late seventies. He is slender with a full head of white hair and bushy white eyebrows. He is a kindly man. He is also sharp as a tack.

Sal sits down across the desk from the doctor and says, "So, Doc. How much time do I have?"

Dr. Birch smiles at Sal and opens a folder in front of him. He scans something there. It is a habit, or maybe a kind of ritual. Sal has the feeling, as usual, that the good doctor has all the entries already memorized.

"Well, all of the tests from your physical came back fine. Lungs good, heart good, everything clear and good. Blood pressure starting to inch up a bit, but we don't need to worry about that just yet. So, Sal, I would say fifty years, sixty at the outside." The doctor and Sal share a laugh.

Dr. Birch leans back in his chair. "But we already knew that didn't we? All these results are basically the same as the last time. You're really more interested in another matter, right?"

"Yes, Doc. What's the word?"

Dr. Birch slides the first folder aside to reveal the one underneath it. Paper clipped to the top of that folder is the authorization for Sal to have access to all of Ben's medical matters. Ben decided it was the thing to do shortly after Sal moved into the Rose Garden.

"Well, I did some simple verbal and written tests. I told him it was routine, did it for all my patients at a certain age," Dr. Birch looks away for a moment and then back at Sal. "It could be something else, but the indications are there."

Sal looks at Dr. Birch but doesn't know what to say.

Dr. Birch goes on. "There is a new medication out they say can moderate or delay the process. I prescribed it right away." Dr. Birch pauses. "Did you say his father had something like that?"

"Yes, but I don't know at what age his started. Did you tell Ben?"

"No. Some of my colleagues do but I've found it only causes further frustration and depression. I tell them forgetfulness is a natural occurrence that comes with aging. However, since his father seems to have had it, he might guess this on his own."

Sal looks at Dr. Birch intently, then looks away. "Goddamn it, Doc."

"I know, Sal, I know."

They are silent for a moment. Sal takes a few deep breaths. Dr. Birch speaks again. "Has he ever told you about his leg?"

"No, just that it was an accident. And you?"

"No. He avoids the issue, as though he would rather keep it hidden. But it makes me wonder. A while back I asked him if we could get something going on a knee replacement, an evaluation anyway, but he declined. And now, well, if he had to go under anesthesia it might accelerate his condition."

Sal's mind races. "So then, what can I do?"

"Be his friend. Be positive, keep him positive. Keep him interested and involved. Get him interested in new things. Maintain those morning walks with him. He's lost quite a bit of weight since you got him moving."

Sal looks away then back at Dr. Birch. "And, as it goes?"

Dr. Birch's words seem faraway, yet heavy as bricks. "Memory loss, sadness, frightening dreams, paranoia, delusions. You may see one or two, or none. And he may begin to sleep more, nod off easily. Some symptoms he may keep inside, no doubt. No one will know early on. Hard to predict."

"So, any idea on time?"

"Again, not predictable. It moves quicker in some than in others." Dr. Birch pauses a moment. "You, being his closest friend, will probably be the first to notice any change in his personality."

Sal struggles with his thoughts. It occurs to him that no one knows Ben the way he was. That the life of a good man went by and there is no one left to speak for him, for how he used to be. "Doc, you see him as he is now, but he was not always that way. When we were kids, he was the sharpest of us all. Back then, I don't believe we had such a thing as 'most likely to succeed' but he would be that person, hands down. We, I, always thought that of all our class he would have gone the farthest. He was bright and smart and witty. And a great athlete. And an outstanding boxer in the Army. And…and he always…."

Dahlia's voice comes over the intercom, saying there are two calls waiting. Sal stands up and thanks the doctor and walks out. He waves at Dahlia as he passes by her desk on his way out the door while she waves bye to him and speaks on the phone. Outside,

Sal struggles with Dr. Birch's words, what they might mean, how it could be.

He walks quickly through the orchard and thinks back to his earliest boyhood memory of himself and Ben. It was the first day of school and he and Ben were wearing brand new clothes. They walked down the trail of the mountain side by side laughing while somewhere behind them their mothers followed.

Sal slows down. He is no longer in a hurry. He walks off the path to a bench nearby where he sits down and looks across to the other side of the orchard. Thoughts of youth and home spring up and pass by. Sal thinks about time, how it moves, the quickness of it.

On a rocky slope behind the mountain called Heaven Hill the original gold and copper camps of Orenville sprang up and grew. On one side of the slope it was said they found pieces of quartz streaked with gold and on the other side a vein of pure copper on a rock face. The camp began like other mining camps in the olden days with tents and shacks along a single curving road. Then it became a small town with one saloon and then a few more of the two-story type. In those days and in those saloons, there was the usual brisk business of selling whiskey in one part of the establishment while the poker games went on in another and in some there was the added attraction of painted ladies up the stairs. The old timers said there were seven saloons but that may have been only to make it rhyme with heaven. No one knew for sure. But early on the gold gave way to copper and copper was what the town of Orenville was all about and the whorehouses dwindled down to a single one and it was not on Heaven Hill.

The years went by and the town grew and spread until the three mountains—Heaven Hill, Crown Hill, and Queen Hill— were filled with houses from top to bottom.

Coming down from the old saloon days and still popular was the weekly newspaper. Ben and Sal sold it house to house on Heaven Hill on Thursdays after school. Ben would take one side of the mountain and Sal the other and it could take them well into darkness to finish. Sometimes they started late because first they had to decide who had which section since the residents of one side might buy a few more papers than the other. It wasn't always the same side, just luck, so the discussion could take a while before they agreed. Then the boys would take a few more minutes to read the sports page and talk about it before starting out. That newspaper was not published in Orenville itself but in the next town, Stanton, which was seven miles down a long winding road.

In the early fifties the most popular sport all around was boxing. The state and local newspapers ran articles and stories about the contests and fighters all the time. Some of the fighters were quite good, others not so good but colorful and the stories in the papers made them even more so. Sometimes, the stories were more entertaining than the fights themselves.

The articles inspired many of the boys on Heaven Hill to dream of becoming famous boxers when they grew up. Those fantasies usually lasted until they found out that going a couple of rounds was exhausting, and also that there was no glory whatsoever about a glove with a fist in it landing on your nose. Then they would change their minds and think that maybe it was okay to just be fans and readers of the sports page.

In those days there was an up and coming young boxer by the name of Primo Paz who was scheduled to fight for the state middleweight title. The reigning champion had beaten all his challengers easily, most by knockout, and was known and feared for his devastating punch. Primo was soft-spoken and hardly talked at all but his manager could and would advertise his fighters and himself at the drop of a hat. It didn't take him long to decide that in order to build up interest and excitement for the fight, Primo needed a catchy nickname and decided "Mountain Man" filled the bill nicely. He then proceeded to get his drinking buddy of a local reporter, the one who wrote the most entertaining sports stories, to write up something about Primo. The so-called interview appeared in the sports section of next issue under the headline: "Mountain Man Born in a Cave." The article was picked up by the state capitol newspaper, probably the whole idea in the first place, but printed there in an abbreviated version.

The reporter said he interviewed Primo while he sat on a stool between rounds of a sparring session with his mouthpiece in place huffing and puffing with some words in Spanish and some in English and due to those impediments there might be some slippage in his translation, not to mention the facts, but he'd done the best he could under the circumstances and the reader could take it or leave it, same as always, no hard feelings, and if anyone still had a problem with it they could take it up personally with the "Mountain Man" himself. He went on to say that after Primo worked a few hard rounds he told the reporter he wasn't scared at all about the upcoming fight with that so-called champion because he, Primo, was from Orenville, the meanest and toughest town in Arizona. And, the reporter said Primo said, the meanest people in Orenville lived on Heaven Hill and the higher up the mountain you went the meaner they were. Primo "Mountain Man" Paz said he lived in the highest house on Heaven Hill and behind his house there was a cave. Yes, a cave, and one day when he was a young boy he accidentally woke his grandmother from her afternoon nap and she told him he was born in it. Primo said it had to be true because then she went around saying it all the time whether she was asked about it or not. He also said it was no big deal since a lot of people up on Heaven Hill were born in caves. Even girls. He said he'd rather not get into describing them or their hair too much except to say if you saw one out in the open it was best not to make eye contact if you could help it. No sir. And, if you saw two or three of them coming down a trail in your direction, better be quick about finding some other way to get were you were going, boy. Primo went on to say that after those girls grew up and got their hair in order and became miners' wives, they were mostly okay. Mostly, but you still had to be on your toes around them because you never knew if they were joking or serious. They had the same look on their faces either way. And on top of that they seemed to have some kind of rule about how long you could look at them. Two seconds tops, a little less if the wind was blowing. Forget about studying their faces. They didn't like it. One quick look and time to look elsewhere, pal. Word to the wise and all that. So, Primo said, if you found yourself in a situation where they invited you into their homes for a friendly chat and a shot of coffee in a cup of whiskey better say yes for sure but stay alert and keep one fast eye on them and the other on the front door just in case. Trick was to be cool and casual about it because otherwise after the second or third cup of that coffee-flavored whiskey, those little chats about the price of rice at the company store could turn on a dime to them yelling out the window at their neighbor that somebody's cross-eyed silliness was really starting to get on their nerves. Same with that frozen smile. You gotta see this one, Lupita, they'd yell. Bring your bottle. Then they'd say, relax boy, all we're talking about here is rice. We can move on to a sack of potatoes if you'd like. Another cup for you? And still with that same look on their faces, like maybe they're joking and maybe they're not. You decide. Yes sir, it took a lot of energy to be around them. Some guys could only take it for a little while and then they would need a nap. Scared? What a joke. Next question, please.

After laughing about the article and reading it again just to make sure, there were those who thought the most amazing thing about it was that Primo could come up with such words and actually say them. Some of the people would ask him to repeat the statement but he would just smile. Primo was a tough fighter indeed and there was no quit in him, but he was remembered mostly for those words.

But the words were not true. The Paz family did not live in the highest house on Heaven Hill. That residence belonged to Doña Pilar Duran and there was no cave behind it but in the next house down lived the Villa family with whom she was related somehow and behind that house there was definitely a cave but off limits to one and all since it was used by the fearsome Villa boys as their clubhouse.

According to Doña Pilar, her husband built that house as a wedding present, but he died early in the marriage and they had no children. This was known to all because she found a way to insert that historical fact in most of her long conversations. She remained sharp and alert and preferred to live alone and it was from the vantage point of that high house that she kept tabs on all the comings and goings of the residents of Heaven Hill. Every few days she would make her rounds delivering and picking up news, rumors, and gossip until by the time she got to Ben's house she knew everything. Then, as she sipped coffee or tea depending on the hour and had a small slice of cake or pie that Ben's mother had baked, she would proceed to tell all.

It was during one of those visits when Ben was a young boy that he heard Doña Pilar tell his mother the story about a lost gold mine back when all that territory was still Mexico. She said that in the year 1839 her father, going by an old map given to him by his own elderly father and using the high rugged mesa behind the town as a landmark and guide, once again found that old mine in one of the canyons leading up to the mesa and how he and his partner, who would turn out to be Sal's great-great grandfather on his mother's side, began mining it again. At some point in time difficulties with the Apaches caused the men to leave and go to the presidio in Tucson where they sold some of their gold and then went on further south to sell the rest of it and hire some men to return with them for protection. For some reason they were delayed and by the time they made it back to the area the Mexican American War had resulted in the relinquishment of all that territory to the Americans. Doña Pilar would always refer to the town and the mountains surrounding the town and the stream that ran behind the town by their old Spanish names. She wore a thick gold cross on a gold chain around her neck which she said was gold from that original mine.

That gold cross fascinated Ben. It was large and shiny and solid-looking. After he heard Doña Pilar's story and found out that one of Sal's relatives had been involved in a gold mine he was always on the lookout for gold in Sal's house, especially on the person of Sal's grandmother. Ben asked Sal about the story and asked him straight out if they had any gold hidden around some place. Sal said they did and that it was in a big trunk buried in their cellar but that he couldn't show it to Ben because his grandmother had put a spell on it, and they could both go blind if they saw it.

Sal's grandmother took on much stature for Ben after he heard Doña Pilar's story. Prior to that he had merely thought of her as old and peculiar. Quite so. But no matter what Ben thought of Sal's grandmother, whether she was merely old and peculiar, or old, peculiar, and possibly rich, she was a rarity for her generation. Sal's grandmother had gone to high school and she was always reading books and she spoke English with no accent whatsoever. The books were paperback romance novels and in the back of the book there would be a page with a list of titles and an order form. Sal's grandmother would promptly select another book and Sal and Ben would run down the mountain to the post office in the plaza to mail the order.

While Sal's grandmother was involved in a book she was mostly all right though still a bit eccentric, but when she was between novels it was a different story. She would read everything in sight—the daily newspaper from Phoenix, the local weekly newspaper, magazines, the words on the cereal boxes, anything. She would get jumpy and the atmosphere in Sal's house would change. Ben thought it was like the feeling in the air in late summer when the clouds got high and thick and massive and had that strange purple color to them and everyone was waiting for that first deafening crack of thunder. Something like that. And it was during those times that Sal's grandmother would start to make quick movements. She would just be sitting there and suddenly whirl around in her chair as though someone had walked by and said something. Ben could never understand what it was she thought she heard but he noticed that her jumpiness seemed to quickly spill over to Sal's mother. On the other hand, there was no jumpiness to Sal's younger sister, Alicia, who considered the whole thing a show for her own personal enjoyment and at times would turn away and laugh and then pretend it was a cough.

It was on one of those strange days that Sal and Ben were sitting on the floor reading comic books. Sal's grandmother was sitting in her rocking chair looking out of the window toward Crown Hill. Sal laughed about something in his comic book and his grandmother spun around.

"You!" She said loudly, as though she had just then realized that Sal was in the room. Sal and Ben looked up at her glaring eyes. It was coming and there was no getting around it. It was always the same thing and it had to do with some problem she had with Sal's face. In her opinion, and much to her great dismay, Sal had the extreme misfortune of being the spitting image of his absent father. She never said you look a lot like your father, or I can't believe the resemblance or you handsome little devil or anything like that. Nope. She liked to say spitting image with a strong emphasis on spit, naturally.

"You are, I swear," she spoke in a strange, crackly voice, "the SPITting image of your father."

Sal's mother, who was sitting on the couch with her foot tapping rapidly on the worn linoleum floor said, "Please, mother."

Sal's grandmother let out a long, exaggerated sigh. She covered her eyes with one hand and let her other hand fall weakly to her lap.

"Please, mother. Let's not…"

Sal's grandmother let her hand slide slowly from her eyes down to her throat and made a sound halfway between a cough and a cackle. "Well, look at him for God's sake!"

And, surprisingly for Ben, Sal's mother would turn her head and look at Sal as though his grandmother had just pointed out some strange looking stranger coming down the road. She would direct her full attention at Sal, the baby she herself had brought into the world, and then they would both study his face closely and intently. Sal would fidget and hang his head.

Sal told Ben that sometimes when his grandmother carried on that way, she would make pancakes for him the next morning. Later, after the same thing happened again, Ben began to think that Sal might have a knack for bringing down his grandmother's displeasure at will, seeing as how there was a chance of pancakes in the near future. Ben thought that was a pretty neat trick on Sal's part.

The next day Ben asked Sal about it. Sal got huffy and denied it and then said he had no idea what Ben was talking about. Then he told Ben that if he had any comics or marbles to trade, he should get going and run on down to his house and get them right away. Ben told Sal sure he did and sure he would, but he didn't have any comics about pancakes so if that was all Sal was interested in, he was totally out of luck. The boys stared at each other for a moment or two, neither one willing to back down. Then Sal suggested that maybe instead they could run down the road to the barber shop where sometimes on payday nights after the men had been drinking in the bar next door, they would shoot dice on the old concrete slab behind the shop. Once in a while someone might lose or misplace a coin or two along the edges or cracks.

No sooner did Ben agree when the boys went flying out the screen door to jump up and over the porch railing, over and down two retaining walls to land on the trail, and on into the early summer morning laughing and bumping and racing each other down the road to the barber shop where on that lucky morning they each found a dime.

6

Ben sets aside the book he's been reading and looks out of his living room window where there is the light-shadow-light of high clouds passing by. It seems to him that he'd been sleeping soundly during the night and having a pleasant dream when he was startled awake by a loud bang. After that he slipped in and out of a restless sleep and heard voices from faraway places coming into his bedroom. Sometimes he thought he was back home and heard the faint music of a lone guitar and muffled singing and later he heard a raspy-voiced man, drunk and heartbroken, calling out a woman's name. There were images like a movie just before sleep where he saw the old town shrouded in sulfur smoke and for a moment he could smell it. Then he saw a long line of old miners, stoop-shouldered and dust-covered, coming out of a smoking hole in the ground. They walked by him without speaking.

Ben rubs his eyes for a few moments, settles back in his recliner, and closes them. The effect of his new higher dosage pain medication has finally taken hold and he feels as though he is floating six inches above his chair. Ben starts to drift. He thinks about the story the old miner told him about the blind mules. How they were taken down into the mine as young animals and used to pull the ore cars. Those mules never again saw the light of day. In time, in the darkness of the depths of the mine, they became blind. When they died, they were hauled out, doused with gasoline, and burned.

The image passes by...*at the bottom of a hill in the bright sunlight two mules lay side by side in flames.*

Ben falls asleep and dreams. It is a dream he's had before. Lately, it unfolds with hardly any variation each time he has it.

The dream begins in darkness and fear. Ben sits on an empty keg of dynamite by a narrow-gage track in a long tunnel. Something of immense terror is coming and he is powerless to stop it. There is the musty smell of the deep mine in the air mixed with the smell of expended dynamite. He can smell the odor of his own sweat. He can see downward until the track disappears, and upward to where the rising track ends at a tiny pinpoint of light that he knows to be the entrance to the mine. There are lanterns hanging from spikes in the timbers evenly spaced all along the length of the track. The lanterns give off a dim, fluctuating light and it is by that light he can see the reddish glow of the streaks of copper along the walls of the tunnel and the dull glow of the rails of the track.

The force of rushing air precedes an explosion as loud as a thunderclap. The blast knocks Ben down and sends him rolling along the track. A thick cloud of dust comes slowly around a curve and envelopes him. There is no sound for a moment and then far away a heavy bell begins to toll. He struggles to sit up. From somewhere deep in the mine comes the braying of the mules. A voice as hard as rock says, *you, all of you, are going to die.* He hears the terror in the screams of a hundred men as they rush up the tunnel towards him. Ben rolls off to the side of the track. The smell of feces and urine are all around him and he is stunned to think that they are his own. His right leg is bent in a strange way, and the pain is intense. He curls up facing the wall of the tunnel and begins to cry.

Ben wakes up, though his eyes remain closed. He tries to open them, but they will not open nor can he move any muscle in his body. He hears the sounds outside his apartment—a plane overhead, a lawnmower, the notes of a piano. Despite a tremendous effort to come fully out of his dream he begins to drift back down.

Once again Ben finds himself in the tunnel, but he is not a part of the scene. He is now suspended in the air, apart from and above the commotion. He is an observer of the terror, although there is no sound. The men cannot see him. Ben moves close, face-to-face, to a man who is screaming. The terror is on his face; his mouth is open wide and strings of saliva stick between his upper and lower teeth. Ben moves away from the man.

He is suddenly deep in the mine where a mule lies on its side, its legs churning as though running. Then Ben moves back again, without effort, to where the men claw with bloody hands at the jagged rocks of the blocked tunnel. The men move slowly, there is exhaustion in their movements. Some of the men are sprawled about but they are not dead. They are face up, eyes blinking, chests heaving, shaking their heads from side to side. Other men sit along the walls of the tunnel. At that moment near the pile of rubble another section of the ceiling falls without a sound.

A solitary man comes walking casually up the tunnel. He is Chinese. He pauses by a bundle by the side of the track and says some words and moves on. He calls out something to the men clawing at the rocks. Immediately the men stop and line up on each side of the tunnel, fifty to each side. The man speaks again. All the men sit down, cross their legs, and place their hands on their knees with thumbs resting lightly on index finger. The man speaks to each one and as he does the man lowers his head and moves no more.

Ben looks at that scene for a long time. There is no other movement except for the flickering of the lights. Nothing happens. He looks down the long tracks at the slow dance of shadow and light the lanterns cast. Then the dim lights begin to move up the tunnel in slow procession as they go out one by one....

"Sal, do you remember the old story about the Chinese miners who were trapped and killed in that cave-in?" The men are having a late lunch in the almost empty dining hall. There are only four or five people seated at tables toward the front.

Sal takes a sip of tea and looks at Ben with a mixture of concern and frustration. Ben had kept him waiting longer than usual before they finally left his apartment and then seemed distant and hadn't said a word on the way over. Sal waits a moment before answering. "I hadn't thought about that for a long time, Ben." He stirs his cup of tea slowly, takes another sip, and sets the cup down. "But yes, I remember. The old timers used to talk about it, but quietly, as though it was bad luck to speak of it." Sal pauses. "They said that the rest of the miners refused to go into that part of the mine until all of the bodies were brought out. But they were not brought out. The company merely sealed it off and made a new tunnel down to the ore."

"When did it happen?"

"Seems to me they said it was back in 1910, or around that time. I really don't know."

"How many were there?"

"Quite a few, I don't remember the number."

"One hundred?"

"No, I don't think it was a hundred, Ben. Maybe fifteen or twenty."

"I think it was a hundred."

"No, maybe…" Sal takes a packet of sugar, looks at it, and then puts it back on the small tray.

"How did it happen?" Ben takes a drink of hot tea.

"Well, it was a cave-in, Ben. It happens in mining."

"Yes, I know, but how did the cave-in happen?"

Sal looks closely at Ben. He is not sure what Ben is driving at. "You're asking me how cave-ins happen?"

"Yes."

Sal is trying to understand the question. He wants to look into Ben's eyes to see if he is serious. Before Sal can say anything, Ben speaks again. "Could be from a blast, right?" He looks down into his bowl of soup.

Sal controls his irritation, first at being late for lunch and now by the subject of Ben's conversation. "Any particular reason why this is coming up, Ben?"

"No reason. Just thought about it the other day." Ben speaks casually.

"So, it just kind of popped up out of the blue?"

Ben doesn't answer. He is now concentrating on his salad which further aggravates Sal. A part of him wants to let the subject go and move on. The dining hall is now empty; a busboy waits by the kitchen door. Outside of the long row of windows in the bright sunlight of the afternoon a landscaper trims a rose bush while people walk by. Some of the women ask him for a flower and he hands it to them with a slight bow. Sal looks back at Ben who is still toying with his salad. Sal shakes his head. He starts to speak and stops, then starts again. "You know, Ben, what you have here is a great idea. Yeah. We could spend the rest of the afternoon in a long and drawn out conversation about underground mining, and the dangers of it, and the ins and outs and body counts from some other damn century. We could, but let's be honest, you don't have a lot of time. None of us do. That's the problem right there." Ben doesn't look up, still toying with his salad. "So, here's the deal old timer. Instead of thinking about some cave-in from a hundred years ago, you should concentrate your attention on the here and now and about how you can get next to the Countess. Tonight. This afternoon. Right after lunch."

A flush comes over Ben's face, but he doesn't respond. Sal continues. "Yes sir, that's what you should be thinking about, my friend. What kind of wine will do the trick."

Without looking up from his plate, Ben says something which Sal can't quite make out.

Sal sips his tea and once again gazes out of the windows at the bright day. His frustration is replaced with regret. He should have let it go. He looks back at Ben who still has his head down. "But it's okay, Ben. Sorry. What the hell, don't mind me."

They eat the rest of their meal in silence. As they leave the dining hall and walk along the sidewalk by the fitness center, Sophie Martel, Sal's lady friend, calls out to them and rushes up and pretends to be angry at Sal. "There you are. I thought we had a date for lunch."

"Sorry, Sophie. I had to talk to a man about..." He looks over at Ben who has begun to walk quickly away. Sal calls after him. "Ben, we didn't walk this morning."

Ben keeps walking and doesn't answer until he is almost at the corner and out of sight. Then he looks back over his shoulder and calls out, "Tomorrow, Sal…or maybe next week, if I have the time."

7

Ben is not sure what he dreamed but it seemed like a long night and when he woke up he felt exhausted. Now Sal is standing by the bed.

"Not today, Sal."

"Is it your leg?"

"Yes, plus my allergies."

"Have you taken anything?"

"Yes."

"Do you want me to bring you something?"

"No, that's okay. If I get hungry, I have food here."

Sal looks down at Ben. Ben looks away.

"Well, okay. But I'll check on you later." Sal turns around and looks back at Ben. "You haven't walked for a couple of days, Ben. You need to keep moving. I'll come back later, and we'll hit the trail."

"Right. Maybe later."

At nine o'clock Ben gets out of bed and takes a shower. He remembers nothing else about the morning until his drug-induced reverie is interrupted by a knock on the door. It is Claire and Sally, and they are dressed in pink knee-length shorts. Claire is wearing an orange top and Sally's is purple. Those colors remind Ben of the grape and orange popsicles of his youth. When Ben first moved to the Rose Garden the two ladies had some kind of active feud going on, but now they are the best of friends.

"I do hope we are not imposing, Ben." Claire moves past him and into the apartment with a clipboard clasped to her chest. She looks around, as though expecting to find some other person there. "But," she continues, "we are on an errand of the greatest importance." Claire places the clipboard on the coffee table. It is a petition with signatures. At the top of the page is the word "banish" in bold, capital letters.

"Please, ladies, have a seat." Ben feels woozy. That morning in addition to his pain medication he had taken one (or was it two?) of the new allergy pills Dr. Birch had prescribed. Then, not quite sure if it is proper, Ben says, "May I offer you ladies something to drink?"

"Yes, thank you. A dash of wine, perhaps," Claire says, to which Sally nods and adds that a dash and a half would be better.

From the cupboard Ben brings down three wine glasses and a bottle of red wine someone had given him the previous Christmas. He pours the wine in each glass and carries them out to the living room.

"As you are no doubt aware," says Claire, after she has taken a sip of wine, "we, here at the Rose Garden, have a long-standing tradition of having bingo games every Thursday night." She says this very solemnly. She takes another sip, a longer sip this time, and repeats her statement about their great bingo tradition.

Ben listens politely as the ladies sometimes talk to each other and sometimes directly to him. The conversation moves along, becoming more animated and fluid with each glass of wine. It slowly becomes clear to Ben that the petition is about a deep and troubling concern the ladies have regarding the fact that the women from the "low-class" retirement community across the boulevard, The Evergreen, have been "crashing" their bingo games and winning quite regularly, and acting in a completely unacceptable manner when they do and that all of that hooting, hollering, and butt-shaking must come to an end, period. Sally takes a long drink of wine and calls those women "that gang of painted prunes." They are not liked, and they are not welcome. Put very simply the petition is to have those "insufferable bags" banished forever from the premises, effective immediately. Ben thinks the ladies may have forgotten that the Rose Garden and the Evergreen are both owned by the same company. They go on tours together, although in separate buses.

The ladies continue to complain about the other women until one o'clock when the wine is finished. They thank Ben for his hospitality and say they must do this again; soon, maybe tomorrow, and then they are gone.

Ben paces back and forth after they leave. There is something in the back of his mind, something he can't shake and can't bring forth. He walks to his bedroom and takes a book from a small bookcase there. He brings it back to his recliner and opens it and then sets it back down. He looks at the swinging pendulum of the grandfather clock on the wall. The term *banish* begins to take hold. There is something about it. He struggles with the thought and then the Spanish equivalent pops up. When he was a boy it was a word that held much dread. He speaks the word out loud. *"Desterrado."*

The word brings with it a memory he had not thought about for many years. He isn't sure about the date, but it seems that it happened in a dark month because it was a dark day. Dark and troubling and sad, and now that Ben thinks about it, a lesson in power. It was the day his namesake uncle, Benjamin, and Sal's father, Vicente, were called into the company office and falsely accused of being communists. They were fired on the spot and banished. Any person banished from the town had to be out of his house in three days. It didn't matter that the people owned their houses, those houses sat on company property. It was only because Sal's mother worked as a custodian at the school that the rest of the family was able to stay.

Ben's uncle and Sal's father left the town of Orenville and moved to California. Ben's uncle would come back once in a great while under the cover of darkness, but Sal's father never again set foot in the town. Sometimes in the summers Sal and Alicia would go visit their father for a week or two. Sal told Ben that his father

38

worked as a truck driver in the town of Pico Rivera. Later on, Sal's father established his own trucking company.

Ben's thoughts about the incident give way quickly to another memory but of a different kind. He closes his eyes as he is pulled back to a place where it is clear and bright, and he is once again running in the sunlight along the roads of Heaven Hill. He is pulling his homemade wagon, trying to catch up with Danny and Sal who have already gone around a curve in the road. He feels the spring in his legs as he runs and the beginning of sweat on the back of his neck. He is thinking of an expression his scoutmaster, Mr. Velasquez, was fond of saying. *Time is of the essence. Time is of the essence.* What does that mean? Ben once asked. It means, said Mr. Velasquez, to move like a bat out of hell. Mr. Velasquez was the smartest man young Ben had ever known. Then, one night, he didn't show up for the scout meeting. They said he'd had a nervous breakdown and was sent away to the state hospital in Phoenix. He too, never came back to Orenville. Some time later, in the early fall, Mr. Velasquez wrote the troop a letter saying he missed them all very much. Father Devlin came down from the rectory to the basement of the church where the scout meetings were held and read it to them. It was a long letter and the boys could not understand all of it. To Ben it seemed to be about a faraway sadness. Faraway, yet coming.

As other bits and pieces of memories of youth move about in his mind a full one takes hold. The clear memory washes over him. It is of the morning he and Sal and Danny beat the Villa brothers to the empty beer bottles at the late-night drinking place on the road behind Heaven Hill. The bottles were redeemable for a penny each at the company store....

The Villa brothers came rushing and stumbling and shouting down the mountain. There were six of them and when they saw they were going to be beaten to the bottles their shouts became howls.

Every boy on Heaven Hill knew that to collect bottles at that particular place was to risk a whipping by the Villas. No question about it. It was their place. Ben gulped as the Villa brothers trotted over in a ragged row. Lupe, the oldest, said, *"Este lugar es de nosotros."* The other five, each a half a head shorter than his next older brother nodded in agreement. The youngest one, Raul, was sucking his thumb and had his other hand stuck in his belt, which was actually a piece of rope.

Danny smiled and answered, "Sorry, Loop, you're out of luck today." Danny was fearless but Ben cringed at his words of defiance. The Villa boys made a sound in their throats. It sounded like a growl.

They were standing in a row, from Lupe to Raul. The brothers all looked the same, light skinned with reddish hair, high cheek bones, and rough faces. They took one step forward.

Danny smiled and spoke again. "Better luck next time, man." It was to Danny's father that the bottles were returned and redeemed in the large basement of the company store. So, Danny was confidant that the Villas would not try to take the bottles from them. Ben was not sure about that at all.

Lupe raised his hand, palm out, and turned away. *"Órale, Danny, órale. No inglés."*

"No inglés," all the brothers said in unison, even Raul, but out of the side of his mouth since he didn't remove his thumb. Lupe scowled. His jaw muscles clenched and rippled. Then he looked directly at Ben and grinned his scary toothy grin. The brothers took another step forward, ready and anxious to get on with the whipping and thievery. Ben held his breath. Lupe glared at the bottles in the wagon for a moment. Then he turned his head to the side and lifted it slightly. Forcing saliva through the gap in his front teeth, he squirted a stream of spit that went flying through the air and landed fifteen feet away. The brothers laughed and looked at him, waiting for his next command. It came with the merest flick of his head. At that signal they all turned away at the same time and ran quickly up the mountainside.

"Heads up," said Danny, as the rocks and curses began to rain down. The curses became more personal until the voices were drowned out by the sound of an ore truck gearing down on a steep incline of the road at the highest level of the open pit mine.

Slowly, Ben comes back to the present. The ticking of the clock seems louder than usual. It has been a long day, and the morning seems like it happened a long time ago. He tries to put the events of the day in their proper sequence. Through the window up in the blue sky he sees a few thin clouds moving along. Over the rooftops across the way the tall palm trees sway in the breeze. Ben gets up slowly from his chair and goes into his bedroom and retrieves the box of old photographs. He finds the oldest faded picture and wonders if maybe the original mining camp was in the same area where they had collected those beer bottles. Another long-forgotten word comes to Ben. Those late-night drinking occasions were called *parrandas*, and he once again hears the sound of distant voices and guitars. He tries to think of the English translation and arrives at *carousing*, but that word doesn't seem to carry the same weight or shade of meaning.

The faces and names of old timers long gone come to his mind. He puts the picture back in its place and stands by the window looking out at the windy day.

Ben crosses the room to his desk and begins a letter to his daughter. The words spring up easily into his mind, but it is with some difficulty that he is able to write them down.

The next morning after breakfast and the brisk two-mile walk through and around the orange tree orchard that Sal insists on, Ben goes back to his apartment and rewrites his letter in ink.

Dear Sara,

Last week when you called you reminded me that I owed you a letter and also that you wanted me to write down some of my memories of your grandparents and the old town. Well, last night, as I was going through some of the old photographs a few memories popped up.

I am enclosing a copy of an old picture of Heaven Hill. You can see where the road in the middle of the picture branches and then curves sharply and disappears around the other side of the mountain. Just before it disappears you can see a long, two-story building. That is the Minero Dancehall. It was the social hub of Heaven Hill. Your mother and I and your Aunt Rita and Nino Sal had our wedding reception there. Two or three houses down from the curve is the Catholic church. Just before the curve you can see two alleys. Our house is the second house up between the two alleys. That is where I was raised. I don't know who took that picture. It was included in all your grandmother's things that were left by her after her death, may she rest in peace.

I think this picture was taken some time in the 1920's. The reason I say this is because at the top right-hand side of the picture you can see that the old mill is still in operation. That is, all the buildings of the old mill are still standing. All of that was removed and what was left of the old mill that I remember as a boy were the thick concrete pillars and the massive concrete foundation. It was interesting to explore all the underground passages and nooks and crannies of the old mill. It was like a labyrinth. I still dream about it. I think it's all still there but then I realize it isn't.

Old Orenville was almost a mile high and sometimes in the winter the water lines would freeze and burst. I had to stay home from school one time to help your grandpa lay new pipe. A very cold drizzle began to fall and then turned to sleet as we worked. Your grandpa gave me his gloves. They were those old heavy-duty leather work gloves. When I think of cold, I think of that time. I can still see your grandpa's hands, wet with the falling sleet, cutting the old pipe away. That, and the vapor that came from his mouth when he cursed.

I remember a Lenten evening when I was a boy when I came home after Stations of the Cross at church. Sal and Alicia were with me. It was very windy and cold, and they came in to warm up a bit before heading home. We walked in through the kitchen door where your grandmother always kept an old towel against the bottom of the door to keep the cold out in the winter. As I turned to replace the towel, your grandmother opened the oven door and took out a steaming baking pan of *capirotada*. There was a stack of freshly made tortillas and a covered pot on the table. Your grandmother's eyes would always light up when she saw young people and she enjoyed talking with them. Soon we were all sitting at the table with cups of hot chocolate in front of us and then she put out extra plates and we all laughed and joked and ate while outside the wind howled.

It was a narrow kitchen. Looking back now I would guess that it was no wider than maybe seven or eight feet wide and maybe twice as long. Most of the houses up there were about the same size, that is, not very big. But they always seemed comfortable. Very much so.

Remembering things like that leads me to think of some of the old families of Orenville who came from mining towns in Mexico. They were recruited by the company back in the olden days. Some of those original families settled in Orenville and some in Stanton. Many of them were connected by blood and marriage. There was something special about those old families. Something fine. Something good and decent and noble.

Just now I had the clearest memory of walking by the meat department at the company store on my way home from school. The butcher was Italian, but he spoke Spanish and I can see him but for the moment I can't remember his name. Sometimes, as I walked by during Lent, he would tell me in Spanish to run home and tell my mother he had fresh *cabrilla* that day. *Fresco, y muy bueno,* he would say. I got the impression that he would set some aside for her. I would run home and tell mom and she would send me back down to the store to buy that fresh fish. It was very good. I'm not sure, but I think it might have been sea bass.

There are many other things I remember and maybe I will add them later on, but I think I should close for now.

I look forward to your next telephone call or letter. Please give Marie and Margaret many kisses for me and tell them their grandpa loves them very much.

Love,
Dad

Ben places the letter in an envelope and seals it. He adjusts his chair back to the reclining position and settles in. Thinking of home and other things he might add to his next letter lead him quickly to sleep.

The bothersome sound of the telephone wakens Ben. The room has grown dark. It is Sal. His voice is loud and cheerful. There is laughter in the background.

"Hey, Mad Dog, how are you feeling?"

"A little better."

"What are you doing?"

"Oh, just sitting here reading the newspaper."

"Listen, Ben, I'm here at Sophie's, and she and Betsy want us to go up to the Sagebrush Lounge for a drink. They asked me to see if you would like to join us."

"The Sagebrush?"

"Yes, you know there is a new quartet playing up there now. They say the lady singer is the real deal and a knockout to boot. What do you say?"

"No, I don't think so. I feel a little, I mean, I think I'll just stay in tonight."

"Come on man, maybe that will perk you up."

"No, Sal. Tell them I'm sorry."

"Okay, I will. But we've still got the games tomorrow, right?"

"Yes, Sal."

Ben hangs up the telephone and once again sits in the darkness for a few minutes and then turns on the lamp by his chair. He adjusts his recliner back slightly and is looking straight ahead when suddenly, for a fraction of a second, he doesn't know where he is. He looks out at a strange place. Then, just as he begins to recognize his own living room, an object materializes itself against the opposite wall directly in front of his line of vision. Ben studies the object. It appears to be a square within a square. The inside square is shiny, and the outside square is dull, and there are small buttons at the bottom. He knows the object belongs to him because why else would it be in his living room? And, he also knows that he knows the word for the object, but it escapes him. He blinks his eyes several times and then a voice inside his head says, *television.*

Ben's mind races. He wipes his forehead which is suddenly damp. He picks up his picture book and looks at the notes by the old photographs. He has to read his notes twice before everything falls back into place. Still, the words seem out of order and not quite right and he begins to revise and add to them. He pauses and looks ahead at the task before him, at all the photographs left to do. He selects another picture and thinks about that moment frozen in time. Ben knows that that photograph, like all the others, has its own story with events leading up to and away from it. Things happened before and after. He knows this for sure but wonders if some parts may have started to slip away.

9

On Ben's balcony under the blue skies of a cool Saturday afternoon Sal's words drift by. "...should have gone with us last night, Ben. That guy on the sax played a rendition of the song 'Autumn Leaves' in a way I've never heard before and then he kind of wove it into 'Windmills of My Mind.' It was something. And that young lady sang with a voice like liquid silver. No two ways about it. Beautiful voice, beautiful eyes, beautiful everything. I think I'm in love."

Charcoal smoke curls up and away from the grill. On the television set through the open arcadia doors a college football game is on, but Ben is looking off towards the mountains to the east, thinking of other mountains in another place where the leaves would start to turn at this time of the year. A clear memory had moved quickly through his mind. He comes back. "Maybe next time, Sal."

"Right." Sal looks at Ben for a moment and then stands up from the small table and walks toward the grill, saying something under his breath. He pours some beer from a cup onto the meat. A big puff of steam rises up from the hot charcoals and carries with it the smell of the sizzling steaks.

Ben lets go of the sudden memory and wonders now if he should mention his episode with the television the night before. He is not sure what to make of it. Ben proceeds in a roundabout way, slowly. "Sal, have you ever thought about memory?"

"What do you mean?"

"I mean, what is it inside your head that chooses to remember some things and others not?" Ben pauses. That morning in bed an image had popped up into his mind. It was a long gray corridor with rooms to each side growing dim and misty as it curved off into the distance. It struck him that each room along that passageway contained certain memories of certain times and if that was so he wondered if in time some of those rooms might become closed off to him. This was followed by the sudden jolt that maybe the corridor itself could become closed off. That troubling thought had stayed on his mind for the rest of the morning.

"Maybe our memories are like rooms in a long hallway and each room...." A passenger jet comes in low, heading toward the airport. Ben waits for it to pass.

Sal speaks up over the sound of the plane. "Still don't know what you mean, man."

Ben waits a while longer. "Memory, Sal. What I'm talking about here is memory, for God's sake, you have to know what I mean."

"Whoa. Hold it right there, partner." Sal moves some coals with a long fork. "What I know is that we are here in this place and time and we are old friends and the sun shines on everything. That's what I know."

Ben smiles and then laughs. He looks up at the blue sky for a moment. "One time, when I was six years old, and I had lost one of my front teeth, Doña Pilar told me that if I threw the tooth into the rising sun with all my might I would have much good luck but only if my tooth disappeared into the sun. So, I got up very early the next morning and waited for the sun to come up over the top of Heaven Hill and stood in the alley by our house and did as she said. And sure enough, I saw it disappear into the sun. I threw it and saw the tiny darkness of my tooth arching up across the sun and disappearing. I had my doubts about the whole thing so I went and looked at the place where I figured the tooth should land, but I couldn't find it. Now, Sal, this memory I can recall with absolute clarity. So much so that I can taste the figs of the tree that grew in the Romo's side yard, which was next to the alley beside our house. And, I remember the pure white milky liquid that oozed out of the stems of the figs when you picked them and how the old people claimed you could use that substance for removing warts." Ben takes a drink of his beer. "The reason I mention this is that even though I can remember things of that sort as though they happened yesterday, if you were to ask me what I did this morning I could not answer you for sure. And sometimes, when I am getting ready for bed at night, I look back to the morning of that day and remember something I did, like get a letter out of my mailbox or some thought I had while shaving, or a bit of conversation I heard, and those things seem as though they happened a very long time ago." Ben looks into his living room at the game for a moment. "Sometimes, I…well, my memories are out of sequence."

Sal looks at Ben but doesn't say anything. He is not sure what to say.

"I mean, eventually I can figure it out but sometimes I am not quite sure at what point in my life something happened. Like sometimes I can remember something, but I am not sure if that event happened before or after another."

Sal looks away from Ben toward the eastern horizon. The Superstitions are big and clear and a beautiful shade of purple. He wonders about Ben's words, wonders what they might mean. He waits a moment and then looks back at Ben. "Do you remember my grandmother?"

"Yes." Ben laughs at the question.

"She was a little crazy, you know." Sal smiles at Ben.

"Well… I wouldn't go that far, Sal."

"Yeah, she was. But I've been thinking about her lately and I think the reason she was that way was because she'd had a hard life." Sal looks at the steaks and then pokes the potatoes on the rack above them and comes over and sits down and lights one of Ben's cigarettes. "She lost her husband, my grandfather, way back in a mining accident. He was loading dynamite into a drill-hole when it accidentally went off. So, she had to find a way to support two very small children; my mother, may she rest in peace and my uncle Frank, may he also rest in peace." Sal looks in at the television where they are helping a player off the field. "She took in washing and ironing and sometimes she would clean houses for the Anglos. Mom and my uncle Frank helped her as best they could."

Ben remembers Sal's uncle. He was tall and handsome. There was a brightness to him, and magnetism. He laughed a lot and never seemed to take things seriously. At age thirty he was killed in a truck accident in the mine. Brake failure, they said.

"Ready for a shot, Sal?"

"Did you already twist my arm?"

"Yes."

"Okay, then."

Ben goes inside the apartment and gets the whiskey bottle and two double-shot glasses. Sal calls through the sliding screen panel for Ben to bring out the chile. Sal has brought six fresh green peppers. They are in a bowl of cold water. Ben fills the shot glasses and places them on a tray along with the green peppers and brings them outside.

They clink glasses and toast the old town and the old-timers. Sal gets up and pours more beer on the steaks and turns them over. The flames shoot up momentarily and then recede back down. He places the peppers in a circle along the edge of the grill. There is a hissing sound as the wet peppers come in contact with the hot grill.

"So, about my grandmother. The other day I was glancing through a Mexican magazine and I ran across the word: *fiero.*" Sal looks over at Ben and says, "Remember that, Ben?"

Ben had not thought about Sal's grandmother for a long time. Now she comes to his mind. One of the things about her was that she had a hard time accepting the fact that besides her children and grandchildren there could be other good-looking people on Heaven Hill. She said the people were okay, more or less, just very homely as a general rule. Ben laughs. "Yes, I do."

Sal's grandmother's favorite word was *fiero.* Ben always thought the word was a polite way of saying *feo*, which means ugly. He thought maybe Sal's grandmother was just being fancy about it. She used that word casually and often. Somewhere along the line someone told Ben that the word actually meant "fierce" and one morning at Sal's house he mentioned that to Sal's grandmother. She looked at Ben with a face full of pity, which was a look she sometimes used and which Ben was pretty sure was an act, and then while glancing up and down between his hair and a spot right in the middle of his forehead, she said, "Yes, son, it means fiercely ugly."

That casual word became more pointed when applied to the Villa family. Make no mistake, her tone would say, in this case I mean exactly what I say. Ben got the feeling that there might have been some trouble between the two families way back in the past. Later on, since there was no way around it, she would agree that the Villa twin girls, China and Rita, were pretty.

There were eight children in the Villa family, six boys and the two girls. Sal's grandmother said there were actually twelve but that their mother kept four of her children hidden in the cellar so as not to offend the people of Heaven Hill any more than necessary. *Ponte a pensar, mija,* she would say to Sal's mother, *que tan fieros no estarán, si los tiene que esconder?* Sal's mother would reply that hiding homely children in a cellar was the most ridiculous thing she had ever heard. And Sal's grandmother would ask, so, have you ever seen them? To which Sal's mother would answer, no, I most certainly have not seen any other four children. And Sal's grandmother would say, well, that just proves they are hidden.

"So, thinking about that word led me to the time I hid one of nana's books. Did I ever tell you that story, Ben?" Sal reaches into the ice chest and gets two beers.

"No, I don't think so."

"Well, if you remember, it would take five or six weeks to get her new book, but she would send me down to the old post office every day beginning about a week after she had placed the order."

"Yes, that I do remember."

"So, I got to thinking one night about how tired I was of having to run down there every day. You remember how we would run down the alley to the road below your house, jump over the retaining wall of that road, run down the hill to the retaining wall of the next road, cut behind the church, then down to the steps by the assay office, under the bridge by the old mine shaft, down another long flight of steps, across the lot by the men's dormitory, past the bank, along that long walkway before you got to the company store and then along the other walkway that ran behind the store, then down those steps between the newsstand and the post office. Check the mailbox. Nothing. And then have to run back uphill all the way." Sal takes a long drink of beer and says, "Man, I get tired just talking about it."

"It was quite a jog, Sal." A memory of a summer's day passes through Ben's mind. The sky is very blue above the tightly packed houses on the three hills of the town, and the ice truck is winding its way up to Heaven Hill. He remembers the triangular shaped sign his mother would put on the screen door of the kitchen with an arrow that pointed to the amount of ice she needed.

Sal takes another drink of beer. "Yeah. So anyway, I get to thinking that I am going to be doing this for the rest of my life, seeing as how one book leads to another. And then, one night, I get an idea. I decide that the next time a book comes in I'm going to hide it. That way nana won't be able to order any more books and all my troubles will be over. I think I've found a way to break that vicious cycle. So, sure enough, when the next book came in, I hid it behind one of those thick metal pillars that held up the bridge by the old mine. And then, I took some mud and smeared my face with it and ran back up to my house so that I would be out of breath when I got there. 'What happened to you?' my grandmother said as soon as I walked in the door. The Villas, I said between breaths. 'What about them?' She stood up with her hands on her hips. They...took...your...book, I said, taking deep, raspy breaths between each word while clutching at my throat. I wanted her to think that they had choked me over that book.

'WHAT?' she screamed. Your book, I said, the Villas took it. 'Why would they do that?' she asked. Well, she had me right there, of course, because everyone on Heaven Hill knew it would be quite ridiculous to believe that the Villa brothers would steal a book, of all things. And in English to boot. Don't make me laugh. Well shoot, I had not thought about that in my plan. So, I had to make something up on the spot. I clutched at my throat for a while longer, trying to come up with something. 'Well?' Nana said. Her face was starting to get red. Well, I said, the Villas said that they stole a chicken. 'What's that got to do with anything?' She said, her voice rising. And, I said, when they tore your book from my hands, they said they needed your book for kindling for the fire to roast that chicken back up there in the hills. Nana screamed, *'FIEROS DE LA CHINGADA,'* and fell in a heap on the couch. Well, my mother came running out of the kitchen and Alicia came running out of her bedroom when they heard all the commotion. 'What happened?' Mother asked. I told her that the Villa brothers had ganged up on me and taken nana's book. And, nana, lying on the couch, sobbed loudly, 'And those little bastards are going to roast a chicken with my book.' 'What?' said mother, and then she covered her mouth and turned away and I could tell that she was laughing. But then, just as quickly, she turned back and looked directly at me. And I started to go through my story about how the Villas had tied a kernel of corn to a piece of string to entice the chicken out of Don Jose's back yard and all that but she just held up her hand like she didn't want to hear another single word of my nonsense and her eyes said quite clearly that I had better get this matter straightened out immediately. Now, I was not about to admit anything and lose everything. No way. So, I put on my bravest face and announced that I was going to get nana's book back from the Villas one way or another, even if it meant sticking my bare hands into the fire or getting my eyes gouged out. I just didn't care. I puffed my chest out, like I was willing to die for nana's book. To which my grandmother, still collapsed on the couch, stretched out her hand to me as though to keep me from going and cried *'Ay mijo.* Your eyes, your eyes.' And mother said to me, just go already. So, I ran down the hill and got the book and brought it back." Sal laughs and walks to the grill and rearranges the green peppers. "And that was the end of my great plan." Sal looks in at the game for a moment. "Except that Alicia wouldn't let me forget it. Every time she walked by me or spoke to me, she would cluck like a chicken. If I asked her a question, she would respond with clucks. She did that for weeks and enjoyed it very much."

Ben laughs and smiles at Sal. "How is Alicia, by the way?"

"Doing good. She retired from teaching last year and is touring Europe. I got a card from her the other day and she sends her love."

The aroma of the peppers on the grill fills the air as Sal turns them. "There is nothing quite like the smell of roasting chile to remind me of the good things in life."

Ben goes inside and grates the cheese and gets the batter Sal has prepared. He pours some cooking oil in a skillet and brings everything outside. Sal takes the roasted peppers and peels them and cuts them open and removes the seeds. He fills the chiles with the grated cheese, dips them in the batter, and then places them in the skillet over the hottest part of the grill.

Ben and Sal drink another beer and then the steaks and baked potatoes are done and the chile rellenos are puffed up to a golden brown. They heat up some tortillas on the grill and sit down to eat at the table on the balcony.

"Thanks, Sal. Everything is done to perfection."

Sal looks up at the blue sky. "We are here in this place and time, Ben."

An old image floats by Ben's mind. His eyes glisten up as he looks away. "Didn't you just say that a while ago?"

"Probably, but it bears repeating."

The sun moves along while the meal is filled with stories about home and old friends and neighbors and which of the families were related and who left after graduation and never went back and who stayed on and who died young. The conversation gradually lessens to only a few words here and there and then stops as the sun goes behind a tall tree a few blocks away. The game on the television is over. The teams have left the field and the announcers are saying their goodbyes.

Ben stands up and moves to the railing of the balcony. He looks out for a while, then speaks to Sal while looking away. "Do you still think of Rita?"

"Yes, and you about China?"

"Yes."

"They were beautiful, Ben."

Still looking away, Ben says, "Yes. In every way."

Sal refills the shot glasses. Ben comes back to the table and sits down.

They take a drink but remain silent for a while until Sal speaks again. "It's funny how my grandmother carried on about the Villa boys, but she never spoke badly about Rita and China."

"Yes, she looked at them differently. She said those two girls were going to amount to something. Mainly, she said, because they didn't look anything like their brothers." Ben smiles. "But as it turned out our brothers-in-law all grew up to be handsome men, and they all joined the Air Force." Ben shakes his head slowly. A faraway look crosses his eyes. "So strange they all died young… heart attacks…cancer…accidents."

Sal stands up and begins to scrape off the still-hot grill with a wire brush. "Yes, good men. May they all rest in peace. When I left Orenville I thought they would always be there, always. And then I never saw them again." Sal continues cleaning the grill with his back to Ben. "Hell, all that sulfur smoke and dust we breathed in. Equal parts sulfuric acid and silica, and who knows what else thrown in. A killer cocktail if ever there was one. So, no telling."

There is still a sip left in each man's shot glass. They raise their glasses to each other and drink it. "How is it that the liveliest family on Heaven Hill is gone, Ben?" Ben does not answer. He thinks of the six rough and tumble boys who grew up. His thoughts move about. Death came quick and hard for the Villas. Like some sudden storm, roaring up out of nowhere, blowing everything

55

away. All gone, nothing left standing. Life is not fair thinks Ben, and sometimes just plain cruel.

He remembers how up on the hill the Villa boys all spoke only Spanish but in school they spoke English clearly and correctly. It was a funny thing. It was true of most of the boys and girls up there back in those years. Two separate and distinct societies. How some of the kids were able to move in and out of the cultures so smoothly.

"The Villas were kings of the hill in our generation, Ben. No question about it. Bigger than life they seemed. Those loud, boisterous, joyful voices silenced and gone. The music they made. The sounds of the instruments and how they sang. There are times I can still hear them. The trumpets and guitars, the voices behind the music coming down the mountain, the sound of a saxophone coming down like honey...." Sal's voice trails off.

Ben and Sal do not speak for a while. A few thin clouds have appeared up high, swirls of pink and gold glow in the setting sun.

"We should go back home, Ben. Now that the weather has cooled off."

"The town is no longer there, Sal. You know that, right?"

"I can't believe that Ben. Just can't. But I was thinking more of the cemetery."

Ben has an image of the old road by the old cemetery and men in white shirts and black ties carrying a simple casket up a steep, narrow path.

"Yes, Sal. It's still there."

During the night Ben dreamed of walking up and down the hills of home for a long time without any rest looking for something but not sure what it was. And then somewhere along the way the pain in his knee crept into his sleep and informed him of a change in the weather.

Ben sits on the edge of the bed thinking of his dream and then stands and walks slowly to the bathroom and gets his pain medication from the medicine cabinet. He goes back to the kitchen to make the coffee and then he pulls back the curtains of the arcadia doors. Everything looks wet and gray and there is water dripping down from the grill that he'd left open. There is the sound of thunder far to the north. Ben walks back to the bedroom and gets his box of pictures. He sits at the kitchen table and searches through the box for a picture of China. It is the one taken on the day Sal and Rita baptized Sara.

China is standing by the pomegranate tree that grew in their side yard. She is wearing a white dress, smiling and squinting slightly into the bright sunlight. In her arms is Sara, wearing a tiny yellow dress China had made for her. The baby is asleep. The pomegranate tree is in full bloom and China and the baby are framed by the deep green of the leaves and the crimson of the pomegranate blossoms. At China's feet is Ben's shadow.

Ben passes his fingers lightly over the photograph. In the background of the picture is the side of Heaven Hill that shows a portion of the Minero dancehall. He remembers that just above the dancehall the pavement ended at Don Albino's store. The narrow dirt road continued from there curving and looping to the top of Heaven Hill....

It was a Friday afternoon and all the flowers and fruit trees were in bloom when Ben rode along with his father up the hill to China's house. They went up to have something on the car checked out or fixed by China's father, Alejandro, who did mechanic work on the side.

No kid ever went up that high on Heaven Hill. It was a known fact that the Villa boys would either beat you up or run you off depending on how they felt on that particular day. Ben was surprised when Mr. Villa came out to the wide front yard smiling. His father got out of the car and they shook hands. Mr. Villa smiled and winked at Ben and told him he thought the boys were back behind the mountain flying their kites. His tone was like maybe Ben would like to run back there and join them, a matter entirely out of the question as far as Ben was concerned. Later, Ben found out his dad and Mr. Villa were old friends and that they had worked together years before in the mining town of Cobre, which was on the other side of the state and also where Ben's mother was from.

Ben's father raised the hood of the car and he and Mr. Villa began discussing whatever the problem was. Since there was no sign of the Villa boys, Ben got out and started to move around the various sorted piles of scrap metal and old car parts. There were chickens running ahead of him as he walked along the narrow paths between the mounds of metal. The different kinds of rusty parts interested Ben. He wondered where they fit in a car and what they did. One of the paths led around to the side of the house. Ben was thinking of what Sal's grandmother had said about the Villa's mother hiding some kids in the cellar. He knew it was silly but a part of him wanted to believe that story because it was mysterious and scary. Ben looked back toward his father and Mr. Villa and heard them laughing and joking. He moved off toward the side of the house beneath the long porch where some steps led down to the door of the cellar. One of the slats on the door was missing. He looked around and stepped down one of the steps, then another.

"What are you looking for?" Ben jumped straight back up to the top of the steps. He looked up and there was China sitting on a cot at the other end of the porch sewing some pieces of cloth together. He couldn't believe he hadn't seen her in the first place. He blushed and hung his head. What answer could he give? He wanted to run away, down the hill.

"Are you looking for the kittens?" China asked.

"Yes." Ben lied.

"Too late. We already gave them all away."

"Okay." Ben said, as he started to walk away.

China was looking intently at him. "Come up here."

Ben walked around and back up the steps to the porch. He had always wanted to speak to China but never had the nerve. He always thought his first words to her would be something wonderful and witty and she would be impressed. Now she knew exactly how stupid he was. *Children hidden in the cellar.* It was all Sal's grandmother fault, and he imagined her laughing at him.

"Sit there," China said, indicating a place at the end of the cot. Ben sat down and looked away, down, toward the mine.

"How come you never talk to me?" China asked, and then added, "Ben."

"Well...I..."

"Are you afraid of my brothers?"

"No." Ben said. His mother had taught him to never lie, and here he had already lied to China twice in twenty seconds.

"Do you know my name?" China asked him.

"Yes," Ben said.

"What is it?"

Ben looked at her to see if she was smiling. She wasn't. "China."

Their eyes met. China held Ben with her eyes. "Nope, it is

Marina," she said. Then she added, "But it's okay if you call me China."

Ben's heart skipped a few beats. "China," Ben said, and smiled at her.

"Do you know my sister's name?"

Ben wasn't sure if China was just playing with him. "Rita."

"Nope. It is Margarita," China said, still holding Ben with her eyes, "and you should always call her that."

Every kid on Heaven Hill and in the schoolyard knew that Rita hated being called Margarita and China knew that Ben knew this. She looked at him with a serious look. Ben started to laugh, and before he could stop himself, he was laughing quite loudly and then China started laughing also. The sound of her laughter made Ben feel as though he could fly.

"I have gold." Ben said, abruptly, not quite sure why he said it.

"Really?"

"Yes."

China looked at him. Ben had never seen such beautiful eyes.

"Yes," Ben said again, "and I will get you some." Without waiting for China's response, Ben jumped up and ran across the porch down the stairs to the road and out of sight. On that afternoon he could negotiate any obstacle up and down that mountain. He went down springing from trail to trail, leaping over boulders and retaining walls until he got to his house. He ran inside and got one of the little cloth bags in which they sold tobacco and ran back out. The thought didn't cross his mind that Sal's gold mine was supposed to be a secret and that he couldn't get gold from there without Sal's permission. Ben couldn't care less about those details. All he knew as he plunged headlong down the mountain was that he was going to bring some gold for China or die trying.

It was fool's gold, of course, but it was pretty, and it had value. It could be traded for other things such as comic books or tops or marbles or just about anything according to Sal.

Sal had found it on a slope between the men's dormitory and the house above it. The ground was a pale yellow and crusted over.

It crunched down when you stepped on it. Ben kicked some of the thin crust away and dug around in the dirt and began to scoop out the fool's gold. He filled the little bag and as he was smoothing the dirt back over where he had dug, he slipped and fell face first onto the ground and cut his lip. Blood began to trickle into his mouth and down his chin. *This is even better,* Ben thought. His imagination flew. He could be the bruised and battered hero finally arriving with the gold to win the heart of the beautiful girl. Or save a town, just like a movie.

So, off again he ran back up the mountain. He was running along the trail below the church, looking down to the ground to see if there might be drops of his blood when, too late, he saw Sal running down the trail toward him. Ben hurriedly stuck the bag in his pocket. They both slowed down. Sal looked at the bulge in Ben's pocket and then at his cut lip.

"What's going on?" Sal said, with a frown.

"Nothing," Ben said.

"Have you been to my mine?"

"No," Ben said, as he ran by him.

"I'm going to check on it," Sal called as Ben ran away.

Ben got to the top of the hill where the road flattened out by China's house. She was waiting for him on the porch. He ran up to her and handed her the bag of gold.

"What happened to you, Ben?"

"Oh, nothing, just a little cut."

China had a small worn purse, which hung from a strap around her neck and from which she took out a single, neatly folded piece of tissue paper. She walked over to the end of the porch where there was a leaky faucet and dampened the tissue and came back and began dabbing at Ben's lip. Ben noticed, for the first time, the small beauty mark just above the corner of her mouth. When she was done ministering to his wounds, Ben opened the bag and spilled the gold into her cupped hands. The gold sparkled on her smooth and perfect skin. She smiled at him and said, "This is good gold, Ben." Just then, China's mother came out to the porch.

"Hola, Benjaminito." Hello, little Ben. Ben had no idea how she knew his name. He had seen her only on occasion when she would come down to Don Albino's store for groceries. Since she always had a couple of the boys with her, he always kept his distance. Now, she was walking along the porch toward him. She was smiling. She had a kind and pretty face, very light-skinned, with rosy cheeks and her hair tied back in a bun. Ben stood up as she approached.

"Que razón me das de tu mamá?"

"Está bien." Ben said, surprised that she would ask him about his mother, and also struck by the way Mrs. Villa spoke. She had a pleasant voice. Her Spanish was rich and soft and strong all at the same time, a manner of speaking that reminded him of how his own mother spoke.

She noticed the surprise on his face and smiled more broadly and laughed. She told Ben in Spanish how time passed so quickly and how the years had flown by but that as young girls she and Ben's mother had been friends in the town of Cobre and how later on her family moved away to another mining town owned by Dome….

Ben places China's picture on the refrigerator door and wonders why he has never put her pictures out in the open before. Other thoughts follow of the kinships and customs of Heaven Hill—the houses, the people, the way it was. All those things seem far away from this city of millions.

The thunder coming from the north grows nearer. The rain means the true start of autumn in the valley. Ben looks out at the low clouds of a gray day and remembers how sometimes in the winter the clouds came down low in Orenville and covered the tops of the hills. When they lifted and the sky cleared up it would get very cold. There were times when the clothes on the clotheslines would get stiff as boards and had to be thawed out inside before they could be ironed. Ben always thought there was nothing else quite like the feeling of walking out into the cold with the warmth of a freshly ironed shirt under his jacket.

A memory comes of a morning when he and Sal joined in the snowball fights all up and down the mountain. They were rubbing their hands, numb with the cold, while they sat and waited at the kitchen table in Sal's house after his mother insisted they eat something before they went back out. Sal's grandmother came into the kitchen just then and in a rare gesture patted each of them on their shoulders as she went by.

Ben looks out at the dark sky once again and has a sudden craving for a steaming bowl of menudo, with lemon and cilantro and buttered saltine crackers. Nothing else will do. He moves to the telephone and dials. Sal answers right away. He says he knows of a restaurant on the Southside where they make menudo both red and white and that it is the best this side of Heaven Hill.

//

The weather has been cold and overcast for three days and each day Ben has told Sal to go on to breakfast without him. The pain in his leg has remained at the same high level, a pain that is alleviated only by the combination of higher doses of his new pain medication and hot baths. Earlier that morning, he had slipped on the wet tile as he stepped out of the bathtub. He managed to break his fall by grabbing onto the sink, but still bumped his head on the round edge of the towel rack. The bump made him feel slightly dizzy. Then, as he steadied himself against the sink, he looked at his face in the mirror and for a moment didn't recognize himself. Later, while standing in the kitchen, his grip on his empty coffee cup suddenly relaxed and the cup fell and broke on the tile floor.

After going back to bed and sleeping for two hours Ben woke up feeling refreshed and alert and the pain in his leg was gone. He looked out of the window and saw that the sun was shining again in a blue sky. Ben got out of bed and shaved and then went into the living room and turned on the television.

Thinking about the matter and turning it over in his mind, Ben decides that maybe fear contorted his face and that's the explanation he settles on. He is trying to come up with an explanation for dropping his coffee cup when he sees Helen walking by. He thinks he should walk outside and call after her and greet her when there is the knock on his door.

"Good afternoon, Ben." Helen is wearing jeans and sneakers and a white sweatshirt on which there is an embroidered golden rose over her heart.

"Good afternoon, Helen. Please, come in."

Helen enters and as she passes by, Ben smells her perfume and it reminds him of the dew-dropped flowers of a spring morning; the red and yellow roses his mother tended so well. Ben sees his mother quite clearly pruning her rose bushes, speaking softly to them. He wonders how a perfume can do that. "Please, Helen, have a seat." Ben makes a motion with his hand in the direction of the couch.

Helen smiles at Ben. "I have not seen you for a few days, Ben. Have you been all right?"

"Oh, just a little under the weather lately, but all in all okay. And you?"

"Very good. My daughter and granddaughter are coming to visit me for Christmas. I am very excited."

Ben looks at Helen. She is an attractive woman. Her medium-length dark hair is highlighted by the strands of silver at each temple. When he first came to the Rose Garden there was the beginning of something between them and it had excited him. But then, for some reason he'd never been able to understand, he felt himself withdrawing from her signs of affection and that chilled the relationship. It had hurt her feelings; he knew full well. And then, although he regretted his actions greatly, he'd never been quite sure how to make the situation right again.

"That is very good, Helen. Maybe I can meet them. I would like to meet them."

"Yes," Helen says, looking straight ahead, "I'll be sure to bring them by." She reaches into her purse and pulls out a letter. "This was in my mailbox. Obviously, a mix up. It is addressed to you."

It is a holiday card from Kemper Stone. Ben smiles. Every year in the fall for the past several years his attorney has sent him a card and a note. Ben takes out the handwritten note enclosed in the Christmas card and reads it.

Dear Ben,

Greetings. I hope this note finds you in good health. Evelyn and I are doing okay, and she sends her regards. We'll be spending Thanksgiving at Sara's, as I am sure she told you. She is a most gracious hostess and has promised us she will come to our house on Christmas Eve. Evelyn adores the twins and is looking forward to seeing them. Marie and Margaret are such beautiful little girls.

Ben, I don't know if I've ever told you this, but I count the day we met as one of the luckiest of my life. If you had not agreed to allow me to represent you, I suppose I might still have turned my life around but who knows? Anyway, to have had the honor to know you and Sara and the twins is something I will always hold dear.

Evelyn and I will be going out to our Scottsdale place probably around the middle of January. We hope to see you often then.

Sincerely,
Kemper and Evelyn

Ben places the note back into the card and puts the card back in the envelope.

"From an old friend?" Helen asks.

"Yes, an old friend." Ben pauses. He wants to say that Kemper Stone came in the nick of time to save his life and renewed in him an almost extinguished sense of hope. It showed him the living proof of men of goodwill, and how men such as those can become a light for others. But Ben is not sure how to say those things. He says simply, "And a great man."

Helen turns to look at Ben. Their eyes meet and Ben is once again struck by their beauty. It is not only their rare golden-green color but in their depths, Ben sees compassion and kindness. Ben speaks quickly, before he has a chance to change his mind. "Helen, your friendship means a great deal to me." Ben turns away, not quite sure if those were the proper words to use. Helen places her hand lightly over Ben's. "And yours to me." Ben takes her hand in both of his and then, unable to meet her eyes, looks away.

"Helen, I am..." Ben begins in a thick voice.

"You don't need to say anything, Ben."

Ben looks at Helen. She holds him with her eyes for a moment, then says, "We're okay, Ben." Ben stands up while still holding Helen's hand in his and draws her up to him. Helen lifts her face, and her lips brush lightly against his and Ben feels something he has not felt in a long time. Somewhere deep inside there is suddenly the promise of spring. He feels dizzy for a second but forces himself to remain calm.

"Helen, would you like to go for a walk out in the orchard with me?"

"Yes, I would love to. Actually, I was on my way there when I dropped by."

Ben and Helen walk over to the ten-acre orange tree orchard that separates the active from the assisted life Rose Garden. There is a gently curving walking trail through and around the thick orchard. The orange tree trunks are all painted white and Ben has sometimes wondered if it might be possible for a person to become lost in the depths of that small forest. He has walked that trail many times with Sal, usually every morning after breakfast, and although he has lost forty pounds since Sal started him on his "regimen," Sal says he still has another twenty to go. Here and there along the trail there are benches and in some places there are also picnic tables. The shiny leaves of the orange trees are a deep green and the rain-washed oranges hang like bright, small lanterns in the shade. On the spur of the moment, Ben reaches up and picks two ripe oranges above the table where they are sitting and as he does a tingle travels the length of his body. Ben hands one of the oranges to Helen who blushes and smiles at Ben. She holds the orange in both hands, close to her chest. Ben takes out his handkerchief and spreads it out on the table and then peels his orange very quickly and separates the sections and places them on the clean handkerchief. He moves the handkerchief towards Helen. "Please," Ben says. They each take a section of the fruit and eat it. The fruit is cold and sweet and the juice squirts down Ben's chin. Helen laughs and bites down and allows some juice to run down her chin also and then reaches into her purse and pulls out two tissues and gives one to Ben. They finish that orange and Helen hands Ben the second one which he peels, and they eat it the same way, laughing. They speak of many things with Ben doing most of the talking, which surprises him. It's as though a gate has opened, and the words come quickly and easily. He speaks of things he has not spoken of to another person for a long time. It occurs to Ben as he is speaking that he has twenty years of conversation stacked up in his throat and each word is pushing the one ahead of it out. He speaks about his lawsuit and the outcome.

"Anyway, I took the bulk of the settlement and established a scholarship fund."

"That is good, Ben."

"It is called the Marina Scholarship Fund. It is for the sons and daughters of miners in the Southwest."

"Marina?" Helen's hand comes up to her mouth and she looks away from Ben.

"Yes, the scholarship is named after my wife. That was her name, but her nickname was China."

"Cheena?" Helen pronounces the name as Ben had.

"Yes. In Spanish the word *china* means the country of China or a Chinese female but a form of it is also used to describe curly or wavy hair. After she started school, most of the kids began to pronounce it in the English way but some of us still said it with the Spanish pronunciation. She didn't mind either way."

They are both silent for a moment. A small breeze picks up. "So," Ben says, "your daughter and granddaughter are coming to visit?"

"Yes. Yes, they are. I can hardly wait." Helen smiles at Ben. "Will yours be coming to visit you for the holidays?"

"No, not this year. Sara, my daughter, says that they will be moving out here soon so she will be busy arranging all that. She administers the affairs of the scholarship and she will be moving her office here to the valley."

"That will be nice for you having them close."

"Yes. I am looking forward to it."

Another breeze moves through the trees. It carries a slight chill with it. Ben takes off his sweater and places it around Helen's shoulders.

"Why, thank you Ben. That is very kind." Helen laughs. "You know, even as a child I didn't like the cold."

"In Minnesota?"

"Well, yes, but even before that in Russia." Helen pauses and looks at Ben to see if he is interested. With his eyes Ben tells her that he is.

"We lived in a small silver mining town in eastern Russia and I remember looking out of our kitchen window all winter long and seeing only hills of snow and very long icicles hanging from the eaves. That is, when you could see anything at all since it seemed to me that there was a lot more darkness than light in the winter. Sometimes, we had to walk to school through trenches almost like tunnels dug out of the snow. I was ten years old when we came to America and I remember the day we left, how the train had to travel very slowly because it would slip off the track so easily due to the ice and then some men would get off and use these large metal things to get the wheels back onto the tracks."

"Frogs," Ben says.

"I'm sorry?"

"Those metal things are called frogs. They have grooves in them to force the wheels back onto the tracks."

"Well yes, you are exactly right, Ben, that is what they did." Helen places her hand over Ben's. She laughs. "So, of all places, where do we come to in America? Duluth, Minnesota. Talk about cold!"

Helen moves closer to Ben so that their arms are touching. The sun falls below the horizon. "Would you like to go back, Helen?"

"To Duluth? No, I really wouldn't want to."

Ben laughs. "No, back to your apartment."

Helen chuckles. Ben feels her laughter against his arm. "Do you?"

"Not really, but the wind is picking up."

"Yes, yes, it is." Helen takes up the handkerchief, folds it neatly, and hands it back to Ben. Ben stands up and offers his hand to Helen. He is surprised at the pleasant warmth of her hand. It seems to radiate up his arm to his shoulder. He wonders about this kind woman who was born so far away, across an ocean and deep into another continent thousands of miles from the place of his own birth. He wonders how two very different lives could come together and one give such perfect warmth to the other.

"Ben, I was thinking of baking some Cornish game hens today and I was going to make some wild rice and a salad to go with them. Would you like to have dinner with me?"

"Yes, I would like that very much, Helen."

As they make their way back to the complex, Helen says, "Did you say that your wife's name was Marina?"

"Yes."

"Well, did you know that Marina is a Russian name?"

"No, I didn't know."

"Yes, it is. That was my mother's name."

"Really?"

"Yes, isn't that remarkable?"

Ben looks at Helen and their eyes meet. He feels a great urge to take her into his arms and embrace her tightly but by then they are in the complex and people are walking by. Helen seems to sense his feelings. She blushes and laughs.

As they part, Ben says, "May I bring something to dinner?"

Helen glances sideways at Ben. The chill in the air accentuates the blush on her face. She smiles and shakes her head. "Just you."

12

At five o'clock in the morning Ben and Sal speed along the freeway at eighty miles an hour heading east on their way to Orenville. Ben looks out of his window to see the lights of the city become less and less numerous until they thin out and end altogether and the blackness of the open desert begins. The radio is playing softly, tuned to a Mexican station. An old song is playing, the kind the old timers used to sing. As the faintest glow of dawn begins on the horizon, Ben and Sal spontaneously sing along.

The song ends, replaced by static and then silence as the radio loses its signal. Ben looks out at the darkness again as his thoughts slip back to the idea of going back home. He tries to not let too many memories rush in, then settles on the memory of his first day of work at Dome. After a mile or two, Sal turns to look at Ben. "You okay, Ben?"

"Yeah, I'm okay, but I was just thinking why we went back. I mean, after we got out of the Army, we could have chosen just about any other place to start a life. Why did we go back?"

"I don't know, Ben. I don't think I've ever really thought about that. Probably, we went back because of Rita and China."

"We still could have left, I think, at the very beginning. They would have left with us."

"I don't know. But yes, they would have. Still, they were pretty close to our mother-in-law, Maria, may she rest in peace."

"Yeah, I guess you're right."

"No, Ben. I really don't know if I'm right or not. Your guess is as good as mine. All I know for sure is that I was glad to be out of there. Later, after..."

"Do you remember the day we started at the crusher, Sal?"

Sal laughs and shakes his head. "Yeah, but I'd rather forget." Sal turns to look at Ben. "It was your standard cold day in hell with a one-eyed character straight out of the movies."

Ben laughs. It *was* cold that morning, below freezing, and it always seemed to him that to enter the plant and climb the steps and go past the heavy-gauge chain-link fence was to enter another world.

A vague picture turning clear comes to Ben's mind. A group of dusty old miners leaving the mill at quitting time...

B en and Sal drove down to the reduction works together. It was still dark when they walked up to the time-card shack where a man handed them each a card and a hard hat and said, "Follow me, boys." He led them across several sets of railroad tracks and around frozen puddles and between some gray buildings where the sulfur smoke hung low like fog. Up above them in the darkness rose the dim lights of the mill. Suddenly, the mill became illuminated with a red glow. Ben turned back to see a train, five hundred yards away, dumping its load of molten slag from the smelter. The men entered a long, dark building where there were several huge canvas-covered wheels turning slowly in large vats that contained a black slurry. The slurry was sucked up against the canvas by means of vacuum lines attached to the wheels. As the wheels turned, scrapers on the other side would skim the steaming black concentrate onto a conveyer belt that moved quickly towards the smelter.

The man led them up a series of long, zigzagging metal stairs and then they walked into the first floor of the mill where above them a long row of huge ball mills turned slowly, and the noise was deafening. Then they walked up another flight of stairs to a place behind the ball mills. There, a concrete walkway covered with a layer of dust ran behind the individual conveyer belts that fed each mill. A long string of bare light bulbs cast individual pools of light for several hundred feet until the lights were obscured by a dusty darkness.

Each belt ran along rollers up at an angle from a sump beneath the level of the walkway to the ball mill itself. Coming down from above were metal chutes which fed each belt. As the conveyer belts ran along, some of the crushed ore would spill back down into the sumps. There were men working inside the shadowy sumps, with only their backs visible, shoveling the spilled ore back onto the conveyor belts.

The three men walked to the end of the ball mills, which ran for a long way, and then further on to the crusher area, past a long rack with shovels and push brooms, and then to a narrow opening that led into a low concrete room like a bunker. Inside the room there was a metal desk, a chair, a metal bench, two doorless wall lockers and a rack with timecards stuck into slots. An old man was sitting at the desk smoking a corncob pipe. The man who was escorting Ben and Sal stopped at the entrance to the room and shouted, "Here's your two men, Sparky." Then he walked quickly away. The man at the table jumped up and threw his hard hat on the floor. He kicked at it but missed and then came rushing toward the doorway. The man was extremely bowlegged. He had one regular sized eye, but the other eye was large and bulging. "TWO MEN?" He yelled at the other man, spit flying from his mouth, "I ASKED FOR FOUR MEN, YOU SONOFABITCH!"

The man smiled at Ben and Sal and winked his large eye. With thumb and forefinger, he reached up and removed the eye and began cleaning it with a dirty paper towel. He reinserted his glass eye and then reached in one of the lockers and took out two respirators. The noise inside the bunker was a deep and sustained rumble. The man coughed a few times and spoke in a raspy voice. "Name's Sparky Blims boys, and I'll tell you like I been told. Eight hours work for eight hours pay. The new work schedule has gone into effect, twenty-six days on and two days off. Time starts when you put your cards into those slots." He put one hand on Ben's shoulder and the other on Sal's and drew them close to him. "Here's the way it is boys. If you take care of me, I'll take care of you." He smiled, showing wide gaps between his front teeth. "Leave your lunch buckets in there." He pointed to the second wall locker.

Sparky Blims then led them back out of the bunker, handed them their respirators and signaled for them to grab shovels and follow him down a flight of concrete steps into a long, dimly lit tunnel where an ore-laden, five-foot wide conveyor belt moved quickly up in a gradual rise until it disappeared. A metal overpass straddled the conveyor belt. There were large piles of ore all along on either side of the belt, and there was the steady loud rumble of the crushers overhead. Sometimes the rumble would change in intensity as a particularly large boulder was crushed. The vibration would knock off some of the dust clinging to the sides and ceiling of the tunnel. Sparky signaled Ben to one side of the belt and Sal to the other and made the motion with his arms of shoveling ore back onto the belt. He pointed to his wristwatch and made the sign for eleven o'clock, which was two closed fists and then one finger, followed by the sign for eating. Then he walked back up the steps and disappeared. Ben and Sal started shoveling the spillage back onto the chest-high belt and worked their way along until the dust swallowed up the overpass. The dust became worse the further up the slope they moved until all that Ben and Sal could see of each other was the dull shine of their metal safety hats. At the end of the tunnel the conveyor belt rose sharply and disappeared into a hole in the ceiling. They walked down to their starting place where the piles of ore had begun to build up again and worked their way back up to the end of the tunnel.

The old picture of the dusty miners leaving the mill fades as Ben looks out at the first faint rays of the sun showing on the horizon. He looks at Sal but doesn't speak as another memory appears. It is of an early summer morning. That morning. That one clear morning when he and Sal and Rita and China drove up to the forest behind Orenville to spend the day. They cooked breakfast over an open fire and grilled steaks in the afternoon. As they got ready to drive back home, Rita and China said that they would drive down together while Ben and Sal and little Sara, who had fallen asleep in Sal's arms, drove back in Ben's car....

Ben looks out at the dawn and tries to move on, tries to find some other memory in place of that late afternoon but nothing else will come. And so it was that Rita and China were driving ahead of them when on one of the narrow turns a truck pulling a horse trailer came around the curve partly into their lane. Rita slowed down and moved over to the shoulder. She had begun to move back onto the road when the car fishtailed. The car went over the edge and down a steep, one hundred-foot drop. Rita was killed instantly. China was knocked unconscious with no other injuries except for a small gash on the top of her head.

Three months after the accident Ben and Sal sat down on a dusty pallet outside the mill to have their lunch. Sal unscrewed the canister of his respirator to remove the disposable filter and saw it was covered with black dust, as usual, and just as usual cursed his long streak about it. "Ben, the dust we see is white or light gray, why do these filters turn black?" Sal threw the filter to the side and replaced it with a new filter from his lunch pail. By the end of the shift the new filter would be black also.

"I don't know, Sal." Ben didn't like to linger on the thought of the black dust.

Sal stopped eating and looked up and away toward the twin smokestacks of the smelter where the huge plumes of sulfur smoke rose high in the air and then dropped back down again like a loop. "Ben, how many jobs do you think we've put in for since we started?"

"I don't know," Ben answered. "A few."

"And we're still here, right?"

"Yes, Sal. But maybe the next time..."

Sal smiled at Ben. "You know, I see some of these old guys working here and I see myself in twenty years still cleaning out that same tunnel."

"Things will get better, Sal. You've got to believe things will get better."

"Well, maybe things will get better around here and maybe they won't. But sometimes I look at those old guys and it gives me a funny feeling."

Ben turned toward Sal and saw that his eyes had glistened up. "Come on man, don't let them get you down."

"I'm okay, Ben. But I've made up my mind. This is no way to live. It just can't be."

An old man came by, hunched over and coughing. The two men watched him walk on and disappear into the long building.

"When you and I were in the army we made a stripe a year. We went in as privates and came out as sergeants. Three stripes in three years. And you and I know damn well that they didn't just hand out those stripes for nothing. Here, we started as laborers cleaning out that tunnel and now it's three years later and we're still cleaning out that same damn tunnel or another one just like it. Day after day. Twenty-six days straight with two days off. It's a joke, Ben. A crying shame joke." Sal looked around and seemed to laugh. "And even if there was a so-called light at the end of the tunnel, we wouldn't see it for the dust." Sal shook his head. He looked at Ben and then away, looking off into the distance for a while before he spoke again. "So...hell, I've decided to go back into the service, Ben. I went down and talked to the recruiter last week. It's all set up. I'm going back in."

Ben looked at Sal, not sure if he'd heard him correctly. Sal kept looking straight ahead. "Sal...no. Come on. You...come on, man. You can't be...."

They sat in silence and looked away at the rising columns of thick sulfur smoke for a long while. Neither man finished his lunch. They would clear their throats as if to say something, but no words came out. The massive concrete foundation of the crusher trembled and shook as a loaded ore train rumbled by on the overpass above them followed by an empty train going in the opposite direction. Sal stood up and then Ben. They looked away from the columns of smoke to the clear, deep-blue sky for a moment and then went back down into the dimly lit the tunnel.

A week later Sal left and made a thirty-year career of the Army. Years would go by before he returned to Orenville.

13

The new emerald-green Buick Ben gave Sal the previous Christmas has climbed smoothly up the narrow canyon pass and over the mountains. The radio has picked up another station, and the sun in the clear sky shines down on the hilly terrain of the open desert. Ben looks at Sal, who is whistling an old tune and setting the cruise control. It will be seventy miles to the next town. Ben settles into the leather upholstery, thinking he might sleep until they get to Farmsdale.

Sal's words sound far away. "Ben, it will be a long drive here. Come on, man. You've never told me the whole story about what happened back home. All I've ever heard is just bits and pieces."

Ben looks out of the window, trying to decide not only if he wants to talk about it but also how to say it. It was a time in his life he would just as soon leave alone. But his conversations with Helen the day before had had a cleansing effect on him. He thinks maybe it's time to get it all out and be done with it.

"It was a bad time, Sal."

"I know, I know, Ben, but…"

Ben reaches for a cigarette and pushes in the lighter. He waits for the lighter to pop out and offers a cigarette to Sal. He cracks the window on his side, inhales the first puff, and blows it out of the window.

Ben begins. "The names of the company lawyers were Tripp, Trammel, and Burns. We walked into the Dome office in Phoenix and there were large paintings of English ships on the walls." Ben stops and looks out of his window, thinking that those words are not the beginning of the story. They are closer to the end. The beginning is mixed up. He struggles to find the string of the first part that will unravel the story the way it happened exactly.

Sal glances over at Ben and sees the confused look on his face. He turns the radio off. "Take your time, Ben."

Ben wants to give up but after a moment or two he begins again. "The strike was on...there were bad feelings all the way around." With those words everything falls into place.

"We were standing at the picket line. It was around two o'clock in the morning. The strike had started a week before and the company convinced some of the men to stay inside and continue working. They told the men they would pay them triple time if they stayed in. The word was that the company had already taken in cots and stoves and food for them. It was bad and there was a large crowd of strikers at the gate earlier but most of them had gone home by then. There were only four or five of us left when John Billings, a supervisor, drove up to the gate with cases of food and blankets from the company store in the back of his truck." Ben pauses, as though waiting for something else to come to his mind.

After a while he goes on. "This Billings was the foreman up at the panel yard which was where the sections of track were made that were later shipped down to wherever new railroad track was needed. The panel yard was behind the highest level of the pit at the beginning of the canyon that led up to the mountain we called Corona. Did your grandmother ever tell you anything about that place, Sal?"

"I think so. I think that's where she told me her grandfather had his mine."

"Right. So, anyway, one day one of the old timers told me that at one time, way back, over a thousand souls lived up there. That's how he said it, 'mas que mil almas.' Now, that interested me very much. So, one day I ate my lunch quickly and began walking up this very old and narrow road that wound its way up into the canyon. Pretty high up on the mountain I saw the foundations of what looked like maybe some type of old mining operation and then I saw the remnants of old houses and also sections of rusty narrow gage railroad track. I didn't have time to look around very much since I had to hurry back down to work. But as I walked back down, I noticed off to the left of the road a flat place behind some bushes. I hadn't noticed it on my way up." Ben glanced at Sal and added, "And I walked into the bushes and saw that it was an *arrastre*."

"An *arrastre*?"

"Yes."

"Damn, Ben, you think that was the place my grandmother was talking about?"

"That's what I thought, Sal. The *arrastre* was the old Mexican device for pulverizing ore."

"So, there was something to those old stories after all."

"Yes. But all that area up around that canyon was closed off since the company owned everything for miles around." Ben pauses, struck once again by the power of the company back then.

"I came back down to the work area and mentioned what I had seen to that old timer. He said that when he was a boy there were still a few families living up there and as we were talking Billings walked by and heard us and then he stopped and came back and asked me what business I had up along that road. He seemed pretty upset so I dropped that conversation and didn't say anything else about it." Ben looks away, starting to drift.

"Yes Ben, go on."

"I…we…used to be sent up to the panel yard on a rotational basis. There had been an ongoing dispute between the workers and this Billings where he had made it a practice to cut their lunch time short or work them a few minutes past quitting time whenever he had a quota to fill. The men had politely spoken to him about it, but he said he could run the panel yard any way he saw fit. That same day he did it again, so we filed a grievance against him. It was an open and shut case." Ben stops talking and looks out of the window. His mind starts to wander. "Maybe we should talk about this some other time, Sal."

Up ahead, a hundred yards or so, a vulture lands and hops toward some dead animal in the middle of the highway. It flies away as the car approaches. A clear image of another vulture in another place and time comes quickly into Ben's mind.

It was sundown, and Ben had briefly fallen back behind the rest of the scout troop as they returned from a hike to the river. The troop had disappeared around the curve of the trail that ran along the side of a rocky mountain. Ben was admiring an arrowhead of white quartz he'd found in a cave in one of the canyons that ran down to the river. Mr. Velasquez told him it was thousands of years old. In the approaching dusk the arrowhead gleamed in Ben's hand. Then, as he came around the curve of the hill, he was shocked to see a vulture standing on the trail twenty feet away. Even in the dark shadows of the mountain the blackness of the bird seemed to jump out at him. Black on black. Ben knew that vultures had to be larger than they appeared high in the sky, but he was not prepared for the size of the bird that stood in his path. It was immense. The huge bird spread his wings, which seemed to make it twice as big, and hopped once toward Ben and they looked into each other's eyes. The vulture hissed. A terror seized Ben, he wanted to scream but couldn't for the spasms in the muscles of his throat. He covered his eyes with both hands, afraid the bird might peck his eyes out or maybe just to shield himself from the horror of that scene. He heard the power of the flapping of the wings and felt the movement of the air around him as the bird flew away. Ben ran quickly to catch up with the rest of the troop. He'd never forgotten the sight of that vulture nor the look in the bird's eyes. Now, Ben shudders.

Sal speaks. "So, Billings drove up to the picket line, Ben?"

Ben waits for the image of the vulture to pass. "Yes, it was about two in the morning and he had cases of food in the back of his truck. He came to a stop there at the entrance to the mine and looked over at me, but he didn't say anything. Then he drove forward a few feet. At that same time, Fred Valle, you may remember him, stepped in front of the truck and spoke some words. Billings stopped again. I was standing behind and to the left of the truck. I saw him look at me through the side view mirror and then...and then the truck..." Ben's voice trails off.

A mile or two later when Ben begins speaking again Sal hears the rest of the story. It is an old story, and, in the end, always a story about two towns. The town where the people went about their everyday lives, working and struggling and dreaming and courting, and getting married and having kids and dying. And the other one where the company's power stood over and above all.

The truck backed up too quickly for Ben to jump out of the way. The impact shattered his right leg. At the hospital the doctor wanted to amputate but a young nurse standing behind him, with the slightest motion of her head, signaled to Ben that he should refuse. After the doctor left, she walked over to Ben and bent down and whispered some words in his ear. She was very beautiful. He thought she said that it would "still be his." He hadn't seen that nurse before, and he would never see her again. As time went on, he would remember her often and sometimes he would dream of her. He was heavily sedated when the deputies came into his room and took his statement.

In a matter of weeks, the strike was settled. Ben could barely walk, and the doctors would not release him to return to work until he could walk without crutches. He exercised his leg every day and when he was able to get around, he went back only to be told that there had been a reduction in force and his job had been eliminated.

"I had always been active in union affairs..." Ben pauses and looks away. The mountains in the distance begin to look familiar. "The union helped me out as best they could, but it was clear that couldn't go on indefinitely. I had already sold just about everything I had, our house, the furniture. I got just a little over a thousand dollars. I sent most of the money to Sara. I went to Phoenix and spoke to lawyers. Each one said the same thing. They were interested in my case but always added that the company had 'good lawyers.' I took that to mean I had no hope of winning. One attorney said he needed five thousand dollars up front, which was out of the question since I had less than two hundred dollars to my name." Ben extinguishes his cigarette in the ashtray and looks at Sal. Sal looks away for a moment, unable to speak.

"So, I went to live with Sara in San Jose. She was working part time and going to school full time. I got a job at a convenience store, on call as needed. It was a strain on my leg, but I kept at it. And then one evening a man called on the telephone and asked if he could meet with me. So, the next day...."

Ben's words trail off into silence. The thread of recollection he'd been following so surely is now lost to him. He is not sure of anything. Confused, he leans his head back against the headrest and closes his eyes and waits for the certainty of his remembrances to return. A part of his memory flashes and fades while another long-forgotten memory about an old side road back behind the town replaces the one he was following, and...branching off from the road to the river down the hill from the old cemetery the narrow road ran rutty and bumpy and rising with a golden color on some of its gravelly curves climbing up among the shrub oak and sycamores to an old abandoned gold mine and Ben can't remember who was with him but they were in an old jalopy and they'd gotten stuck twice in the sand of a ravine along the way....

After a minute or two Ben opens his eyes. "I don't...I...memory is a funny thing, Sal." As he speaks, other thoughts of other times have begun to form in his mind. Something about a cold gray day and a long wait and somewhere something about laughter.

Sal looks over at Ben. He has turned away, looking out of the side window to the mountains on the southern horizon. Sal waits. He will not disturb Ben's reverie. A mile or so later he sees that Ben is facing forward and has fallen asleep.

14

The cold ocean wind came in gusts on that late October afternoon as Ben sat and waited on a chair on the porch. Looking down toward the end of the street, he saw a man appear over the scraggly hedge along the sidewalk. He was thin and middle aged and struggling against the wind. He approached and called out to Ben, asking him if he was Mr. Medina.

Ben studied the man. He was wearing a dark, threadbare suit. The collar of his white shirt was frayed, and his tie was wrinkled below the knot as though at one time it had belonged to a bigger man. Ben thought the man looked like some kind of skid row individual who had cleaned up at the local Salvation Army in order to get a much-needed hot meal.

"Yes, I am Ben Medina."

The man walked up onto the porch and smiled and offered Ben his hand. "My name is Kemper Stone, attorney-at-law. It is a pleasure to meet you, Mr. Medina." The man spoke with a New England accent. He looked deeply into Ben's eyes, looking for something that Ben could not be sure of. The strength of the man's handshake surprised Ben.

"Would you like to come inside, Mr. Stone?"

The man seemed to shiver. "Yes, thank you, Mr. Medina."

Inside, in the warmth of the kitchen, Ben introduced the man to Sara and the three of them spoke briefly of the weather. Sara placed cups and saucers on the kitchen table and served the men coffee. Then, the man fixed Ben's eyes with his own and began speaking. Ben listened to the man in the shabby suit tell the story of a man who had lost everything to alcohol. Then the man said, "What I must add to that cheerless tale is that in my case I always seemed to know, even as I achieved grand successes and dined in the finest restaurants, that I would one day wake up face down in some gutter far from home. You see, that same thing happened to my father. It was almost like a voice inside my head insisting that that too was to be my destiny."

The man straightened up and continued. "I had no idea how I ended up in that gutter. I had an apartment on the other side of town and try as I might I could not account for the week prior to that morning. I had lost my wallet and didn't have a single cent in my pocket. I sat on the curb, hungry and cold and confused. In the faint morning light, I saw an old Mexican man walking by on his way to work with a lunch bucket in his hand. He looked down at me in all my squalor and without saying a word opened his lunch bucket and handed me an egg and potato burro wrapped in wax paper. It was still warm. I will never forget that man's face, and I wondered if perhaps he was an angel sent my way." Mr. Stone paused, as though he wanted to say much more but then only said, "There is more to life than meets the eye, I must say."

Mr. Stone looked out of the window at the brown leaves blowing by. He went on. "Six months ago, on that morning, I finally hit bottom. I have not had a drink since then." He paused and took a drink of his coffee, then another.

"I knew I couldn't simply walk into some attorney's office and ask for a job. I had not practiced law for five years. Indeed, if someone had offered me a job as a lawyer, I would not have taken it. So, I went to the employment office and saw a listing for a courier, which is really a delivery driver, and I applied. I was given the job on the condition that I could get a union card. I went to the union hall and as I was waiting to be interviewed, I was glancing through some magazines when I came across a union newsletter. It was an old issue, from four or five years ago. In it was an article about you, Mr. Medina, which was interesting but that was not the first thing that caught my attention. What caught my attention was the name of the company you worked for. You see, the corporate offices for the Dome Corporation and the legal firm I worked for were in the same building in New York City. In fact, our international department had assisted in some acquisition work for Dome."

At the mention of the name Sara stiffened and her face filled with color. Ben tried not to show his feelings, not so much to repress his bitterness but to restrain hope.

Mr. Stone noticed the change in Sara. He said, "Yes, of course, I understand. But please, if I may be allowed to continue without speaking that name?"

The man gave Ben a sad smile and nodded his head slightly at Sara. "In my long fall to that gutter I had forsaken all of my friends but not all of them had forsaken me. I began reaching out again and to my great surprise one of my old friends had continued my membership to the bar so that my license to practice had never lapsed. I made a few calls and found out that you, Mr. Medina, had not pursued your case." Mr. Stone again looked deeply into Ben's eyes.

"I was told the company had good lawyers." Ben felt the inadequacy of his words.

Mr. Stone considered Ben's statement. He spoke slowly and carefully. "Be assured that D… that is, the company in question, takes great pains to cultivate that reputation. I am quite sure you are not the first person to be defeated before you can even begin to fight based on a mere impression of invincibility."

The kitchen was silent. No one spoke for a few moments. There was only the sound of the wind and the rattle of a loose rain gutter.

"Now," Kemper Stone said, "will you allow me to represent you in this matter?"

Many things ran through Ben's mind, and his heart seemed to falter for a second or two. He remembered the dark days when his world had been turned upside down. Ben looked at Sara. She shrugged.

"I have no money, Mr. Stone."

"None is asked of you, Mr. Medina."

"What do I need to do?"

"You need to say yes first of all and help a man take the first step on his long road to redemption."

"Yes," Ben said, "my answer is yes."

They shook hands. Mr. Stone removed a new, legal-size notepad from his briefcase. "Please tell me exactly what happened on that night, Mr. Medina." The man sat with his pen poised on the pad. Sara stood up and excused herself and walked out of the kitchen.

It seemed to Ben that he had relived that night a thousand times. His words came easily. "It was on the night of July the seventh. The strike was a week old. I was on the picket line along with several other strikers—"

"Their names please, Mr. Medina."

Ben recited the names and then continued. "One week before, on the thirtieth of June at midnight, at which time the old contract expired, the company persuaded some workers to remain inside the gates, promising them round the clock pay if they would stay. The company brought in truckloads of bunks, cooking stoves, and food.

"A man by the name of John Billings, a supervisor, drove up to the picket line in a company truck. In the back of that pickup truck were cases of food. A striker, Fred Valle, stepped in front of the truck, grabbed his crotch, and said, 'I've got something you can take into those sons of bitches, John.' I was standing behind the truck, on the driver's side…"

The windy afternoon moved on as Mr. Stone's questions slowly brought forth Ben's story of the sequence of events of that night in July. When Mr. Stone was finished writing Ben's last words, he placed his pen down on the notepad. There was a look of disbelief on his face. Then he began to slowly rub his eyes. To fill in the silence Ben began speaking again.

"All of Orenville is private property so that the deputies, while selected by the county sheriff, were actually approved by the company."

"I see."

"One day, when I was a boy, I happened to be in the drugstore when the deputies were there. They were drinking coffee and having a slice of pie. They didn't pay for that. They walked over to the counter where there was an open display of cigarettes and candy and gum. They each got a pack of cigarettes and a pack of gum and a couple of candy bars for which they didn't pay either. All the while they were laughing and joking with the proprietor. That seemed strange to me at the time. It is an impression that has remained with me. The reason it struck me so was that it had been just a week before that one of my classmates, Johnny Blue, who was Apache, was caught trying to sneak into the theater. They called the deputies on him. The movies cost sixteen cents back then. Those same deputies came and roughed him up and handcuffed him and hauled him off to jail. No one said anything."

Mr. Stone winced and began writing again. His questions began to go off in other directions, some of which Ben was unsure of their purpose. The notepad became filled with names, dates, and details all in chronological order and perfect penmanship. When he was finished, Mr. Stone went back and checked each entry. He asked Ben once again to verify each item regarding the night in question. Then he placed the notepad in his briefcase and crossed his hands on the table.

Mr. Stone frowned and shook his head. "I am almost at a loss for words." He looked at Ben for a long moment. He began to speak and fell silent and then began again. "Nevertheless, it must be said and said clearly. Here, we have a dimension of moral irresponsibility unlike any other I've ever seen. And, more troubling, it seems to be long-standing and deeply ingrained. It is appalling, and indefensible."

Mr. Stone glanced away again out of the window and then went on. "Having said that, however, does not mean we will prevail in a court of law. I make no guarantee to you in that regard. What I will guarantee, Mr. Medina, is that they will know they've been sued, and exactly why. They will most certainly know that. And I will add one other thing, if I may." A different look appeared on Mr. Stone's face, indignation, a flash of anger. "I know that company well. They enjoy a good reputation in New York City. As a rule, they tend away from publicity. They'll accept it if it serves their purposes, but anything less than that they find quite distasteful, if not abhorrent."

Mr. Stone left at dusk, leaving Ben with a mixture of hope and doubt. A week went by and then a second week and close to the end of the third week Ben began to feel the old despair. He thought that perhaps Mr. Stone had merely been going through a period of sobriety and lucidness but that he had, in the end, fallen off the wagon. Ben struggled against the gloom. And then, finally, the call came.

Mr. Stone's voice sounded strong with a hint of excitement. He said he'd been busy reconnecting with some of his old attorney friends and apologized to Ben for not calling sooner. He said he was sending two copies of the lawsuit, one for Ben to keep and the other to sign and return to him by return mail if possible. He read to Ben the long list of individuals he would subpoena for depositions including Billings, the deputies, the sheriff, the doctor, the mine superintendent all the way up to the president of the company.

When Ben received the copies of the lawsuit, he quickly glanced through the one Mr. Stone had asked him to sign while Sara read the second copy. Ben heard the disbelief in Sara's voice. "Dad, Mr. Stone is suing the company for four and a half million dollars."

During the next three months, Ben saw little of Mr. Stone although they did speak on the telephone every couple of weeks or so. Mr. Stone told Ben of the various legal aspects and maneuverings about which Ben understood little. And then one day he told Ben that the company's attorneys had offered to make available at the attorneys' Phoenix office all of the Orenville individuals who were to be deposed by Mr. Stone if Ben would present himself for a deposition at that same office on any day in the month of March convenient to both parties.

It was the moment Ben had long waited for. He thought he should feel better but instead he had trouble breathing and his heart raced. He had the clear image of waiting at the entrance to the mine on that summer night before his world changed, as the green company truck with Billings at the wheel appeared around the curve and came slowly up the hill.

On the day before the appointment, Mr. Stone rented a car and he and Ben drove to Phoenix together. There was a change in Mr. Stone's appearance. He had apparently gained all his old weight back and Ben noticed that Mr. Stone was not naturally thin at all but rather muscular. During the long trip he and Ben spoke of many things and Ben was surprised at how much Mr. Stone had learned about the Dome Corporation, all the way back to when the two original partners had first ventured into the copper mining business back in the 1880's and how it had been handed down father to son since then. Mr. Stone also told Ben that he and his ex-wife had reestablished a relationship and it was she who had lent him the money to get started again. Ben learned that Mr. Stone's ex-wife lived in San Francisco and was quite wealthy. Mr. Stone told Ben that years before, while they were still married, his father-in-law had passed away and left her and her brother a chain of newspapers throughout the Midwest.

"Ben, the men who will be asking you questions tomorrow know we have a strong case. However, they have no choice in the matter but to go ahead with this in the hopes they might find a tiny thread with which to unravel it. Or, lacking that, just scare you off. Now, there might be a flaw I may have overlooked, although I'm confident I haven't. And, I am quite certain they will play hardball with you in search of that flaw. I know two of these men. We did some work together back east, as I may have told you, and we traveled in the same social circles. I don't believe I've met the third one. The way that company likes to play it is if you have one lawyer, they have two, or three in this case, if you have two, they have four and so on. One of the first things I discovered about them is that they spare no expense in their legal pursuits, going all the way back to their beginning in the mining business in the 1880's. And, in view of all that, I suspect there might be a skeleton or two in that company's closet here and there. In fact, I would bet on it. In any event I will be there to protect your interests. Answer their questions truthfully. You will be under oath. But answer their questions in as few words as possible and do not volunteer any additional information whatsoever. If you do not know the answer to a question simply say, I don't know."

Ben hadn't brought his wheelchair on the trip. He decided it would be too cumbersome to load on and off the car. He had brought his crutches but elected to leave them in the car when he and Mr. Stone arrived at the building where the attorneys were waiting. He limped along, trying to ignore the pain as they entered the elevator and rode up to the eleventh floor. Ben was wearing a suit, but it was old and out of style and a bit too heavy for the warm Phoenix weather.

Ben and Mr. Stone stepped from the elevator onto the plushest carpet Ben had ever walked on. It was thick and firm and sky-blue and smelled new and eased the pain of his walking. Ben and Mr. Stone walked through a set of rippled-glass doors and into an area with chairs made of thick, highly polished mahogany. On the paneled walls were large paintings of English sailing ships plowing through frothy, blue-green waves. On a stand at the end of the room there was an American flag. Ben was suddenly very thirsty, his tongue felt thick. He could feel his breakfast stuck halfway up his chest, refusing to go down.

At a desk next to the flag sat a pretty young woman who eyed them coldly as they approached. She offered no greeting. Then, and seemingly in reaction to her coldness, Mr. Stone stepped up and spoke to her in a tone that Ben had not heard him use before. The words were the same as Ben might use in polite introduction but those same words from Mr. Stone carried the weight (in a manner Ben could not pinpoint) of a superior addressing a subordinate. The result was sudden and unmistakable. The young woman lowered her eyes as a hint of color came to her cheeks. She pressed a button on the intercom and spoke into it.

After a few moments a man dressed in a perfectly tailored three-piece suit came out of a set of massive double doors that extended from the floor to the ceiling.

"Mr. Stone, so good to see you again." The man and Mr. Stone shook hands.

"Thank you, Mr. Trammel. How have you been?"

Ben looked at the man. He had thought often of the "company lawyers" during the years after his injury. He had imagined such men to be fat and soft with sneering faces, or, sometimes he thought of them as thin, vulture-like old men, but in each case, he envisioned them as evil. Nothing could be further from either of those images. This man was of an athletic build, tall and robust, and moved with an easy power across the room.

"Mr. Trammel, I would like you to meet Mr. Medina." The man turned toward Ben and it was then that Ben caught the hard glint in his eyes. It was clear the man harbored no goodwill for any adversary of the company and his tone, while polite, was the same one that Mr. Stone had used on the secretary.

The man led them into a conference room where there were two men sitting at a long table. In one corner of the room sat a woman at a small desk with a small machine in front of her.

Mr. Trammel spoke. "Mr. Stone, you remember Mr. Tripp, here."

"Yes, of course. Hello counselor."

"Good to see you, Mr. Stone." The man stood up and shook Mr. Stone's hand. This man also looked very fit to Ben. A shorter version of the first attorney.

Trammel paused a moment, as though there should be a moment of silence before he introduced the third man. He spoke with deference. "And this is Chan Burns. I don't know if you've met him before."

The third man spoke. "A pleasure." He said this without expression and without rising as he extended his hand. Although he was as impeccably dressed as the other two there was something different about him. What Ben saw was a rawboned street fighter dressed up in a three-piece suit. Instinctively, Ben looked at the man's hands, expecting to see the grime under his fingernails. The man noticed this, and his eyes locked into Ben's for a fraction of a second. The man's eyes were the palest shade of blue, so pale they seemed transparent. He had the look of a man who would do anything to win a fight. This man did fit Ben's image.

"Likewise," Mr. Stone said, as he shook the man's hand. "Gentlemen, this is Mr. Medina." The men acknowledged Ben with a slight nod of their heads.

Mr. Trammel spoke. "Before we get started, would you gentlemen like some coffee or something to drink?" Mr. Stone turned to Ben. "Water," Ben said.

"Water will be fine thank you, Mr. Trammel."

As though on cue at that moment a young black lady, apparently from the restaurant on the first floor since she was wearing a black and white uniform, brought in a small table on wheels with two pitchers of water, a pot of coffee, and a tray with assorted pastries. She turned and walked back toward the door and began to open it. No one spoke. Thinking that someone should say something, Ben turned to her and said, "Thank you, miss." The young girl turned back and smiled at him and said, "You are quite welcome, sir."

Mr. Stone stood up and walked to the table and brought back two glasses of water. Ben took a long drink while Mr. Stone placed his glass to the side. The man with the eyes of ice turned to Mr. Trammel and spoke in a casual drawl. "Maybe Mr. Stone would like a spot of Mexican rotgut to color his water."

Ben sat up. In that moment he knew the old thing was in the room after all. The thing that flags and three-piece suits couldn't hide. The air in the room changed, and there came to Ben's mind the clear memory of coming around the bend of the old rocky trail to the shock and fright of that huge vulture blocking his way. In the silence of the room that followed, Ben thought he might feel the old unease or despair. Instead, he felt the heat of an old fire.

Now he now looked closely at Burns, looked at him man to man without the barrier of status or station and felt the confidence of his own strength. This man, thought Ben, would want to strike quickly with elbows and knees. Quick and fast and dirty was his style. Ben had known that kind before and knew also that if you could keep your head and withstand that first furious attack, he would tire.

Ben looked away, out through the long row of windows to a view of the city from eleven stories high and then back again at those suited men who had the power to change lives with the stroke of a pen. Then, from some other place, he heard the faint sound of a bell.

Ben drifted, leaving the scene, drawn away by some reflex or instinct back to the smell of canvas and leather and the roar of the crowd. Back to the ring where one fighter, alone and ready, studies the other before the first bell sounds. To the moment of extreme clarity and rising fear where everything else is blocked out. To the place where the vision of a plan comes by of its own accord and the world slows down....

...and then, the joining in the bright white heat of the center of the ring and the fury of leather pounding flesh and the waiting inside the center of that soundless storm for the opening to reveal itself, and then the precise explosion of power to the exact right spot and the give of the other man's ribs, and the shock, and the glazed-eye look, pleading, with fear at the edges, and the wave going down to the dip of the knees, to the fall, to the end...

A small smile came to Ben's face.

Then he heard Mr. Stone's voice in yet another tone he had not heard before.

"Mr. Trammel, please extend my thanks to Mr. Burns for his hospitality and thoughtfulness. I have traveled five years and eight hundred miles to be here and expected nothing less." Mr. Trammel blinked several times at the tone of Mr. Stone's voice and at the same time the color came up to Burns' neck.

Mr. Stone continued, still speaking directly to Mr. Trammel. "Also, please advise Mr. Burns that I shall be happy to return the favor the next time we meet."

At this, Burns turned his face toward Mr. Stone and said coldly, "It will be a pleasure."

Looking past Burns, and still directing his words to Mr. Trammel, Mr. Stone said, "Please assure Mr. Burns that the pleasure will be entirely mine."

And then, to Ben's surprise, Mr. Trammel's Adam's apple bobbed up and down in a visible gulp. He coughed in an attempt to cover it up. Then he cleared his throat and spoke with a slight hoarseness in his voice. "Well then, should we get started?"

Ben was directed to approach the court reporter and be sworn in. Then he returned to his chair and the questioning began. After the first few questions, in which Mr. Trammel and Mr. Tripp would alternate, it became evident to Ben that their intent was to confuse and frustrate him. So, he began pausing before responding to their questions as though thinking carefully about his response. Ben did this with even the simplest of questions. The attorneys' impatience began to show through.

Finally, Mr. Trammel turned to Mr. Stone and said, "Please advise your client that these questions are simple ones and do not require such a great deal of thought."

Mr. Stone's voice now had a teasing quality to it. "If you prefer, Mr. Trammel, I can answer for him."

The questions continued. They would move away from the night in question and then back to it again and again. Burns didn't ask any questions. Mainly, he only stared at Ben the entire time with his cold eyes. It was a look of disdain. It was the look of contempt Ben remembered from his youth.

The next day Mr. Stone brought to Ben's hotel room several newspapers from different cities including one each from San Francisco, Chicago, and New York City. In each of the business sections of the newspapers there was an article from the Associated Press. The article was about the Dome Corporation, about its history in copper mining. It was a positive article. The article spoke of the astuteness of the company in surviving and thriving in economic fluctuations. This, the article stated, was due to the high degree of business acumen possessed by the board of directors of the corporation. Ben knew what the article meant and how it had gotten into print. It was a message loud and clear. Dome had been served notice that publicity was available, and it could be either good or bad.

One week later, after Ben and Mr. Stone returned to California, the company made an offer of $750,000 to settle out of court. Mr. Stone presented the offer to Ben.

"What do you think, Mr. Stone?" Ben asked.

"I think it is unworthy of your consideration."

"So, we should say no?"

"Not only should we say no but I recommend that we advise my esteemed colleagues and the gentlemen who sign their paychecks that we intend to amend the lawsuit to ten million dollars and that you consider their offer an insult to your intelligence and that we very much look forward to discussing the entire matter, right down to the smallest sordid and scandalous detail, in open court." Mr. Stone smiled at Ben.

There then followed a series of telephone calls between Mr. Stone and the company lawyers that Mr. Stone told Ben was like a game of poker. Two weeks later a written offer of settlement arrived in which the company would agree to three million dollars, plus an offer of the purchase of a medical insurance policy for Ben to remain in effect for the rest of his life. The only stipulation was that Ben could never speak of any detail of the settlement and if he agreed to the offer, he was to submit a sworn statement to that effect to the company. Ben read the offer and placed it on his lap.

"Mr. Stone, do you think the president and the board of directors of the company know about this offer?"

"Rest assured."

"So, they would have to approve a counteroffer?"

"Definitely. You are suing the corporation and the settlement will have to be agreed upon by each member of the board of directors including the president."

"So then, is it too late to make one other demand?"

Mr. Stone looked at Ben with a puzzled look on his face. "Ben, I am at your command. If this offer is not completely satisfactory to you, we can decline."

"Well, I agree to the dollar amount and the insurance policy but there is just one other thing."

"Yes?"

"I would like the final offer to show three separate items." Ben thought for a moment, not sure if Mr. Stone would understand. "I would like the items to be shown as follows: One, the dollar amount. Two, the health insurance policy. And three, one bottle of Mexican rotgut whiskey."

Mr. Stone blinked his eyes and looked at Ben for a moment. Ben had never heard him laugh before. The sound began deep in his chest and rumbled up and burst out in all its fullness into the room. Ben smiled. Mr. Stone came around the desk and shook his hand. He was silent for a moment, then started laughing again joined by Ben

16

With occasional lapses along the way and a short nap in between Ben is able to finish his story. There are some things that escape him but mostly it is a complete account. When he is done, he says to Sal, "There is a rest stop up ahead. I need to stretch my legs." Sal slows down and pulls off the highway and comes to a stop by the remains of an old ramada. Ben steps out of the car and begins to walk away along a clearing of the desert by the side of the road. Sal watches him walk off and just about the time he is ready to call out to Ben to come back, he turns and heads back toward the car. He is smiling. "Sal, there was something to the old town, right?"

"There will never be another like it." Sal pauses for a moment, looking off into the distance. "Sometimes I'll think of someone, some old character will pop up into my mind, and I wonder what became of that person."

"Well, we might see some of those names when we get there, Sal. Most of those old timers are buried up on that hill by now. May they all rest in peace."

Sal pulls back onto the highway and then quickly accelerates up to and slightly past the speed limit. Ben starts to slip back into his memories. Sal glances over at him and sees again the beginning of the dreamy, faraway look that sometimes comes over his face. Sal begins telling stories to pass the time and keep Ben occupied. Slowly, Ben's attention is drawn to Sal's words.

"…and Danny and I were sitting in the shade of the mulberry tree there by the shoe repair shop doing nothing when we saw this old truck come coughing up the road that led to the mine. I don't know where you were that day, Ben." Sal looks at Ben and smiles. "Probably down the hill stealing gold from my mine. Yeah, anyway, the old truck turns on the road that ran below your house and starts towards us and then pulls up to where Danny and I are sitting where the truck backfires a few times and then stops. There's a faded hand-painted sign on the side of the truck that says, 'Valley Produce Company.' This old guy leans out the window and asks us if we would like to earn some money. The back of the truck is loaded with all kinds of vegetables, corn and green chile and some other things. Sure, Danny and I answer at the same time. Well, okay, the man says. I'll pay you a dime for every fifty cent's worth of vegetables you sell. Did I ever tell you that story, Ben?"

Ben thinks that Sal probably has told him that story at one time or another but he's not quite sure, so he shakes his head and answers, "I don't think so."

"Okay, so the man tells us to hop on and he follows the road back around by the bar and the bakery and down to the plaza and then up the road to Queen Hill. Now, if you'll recall, you and I knew everyone on Heaven Hill, but we didn't have much to do with the people on any of the other mountains in Orenville, especially Queen Hill because all those people were strange and seemed to be related in some way or another and a few of them were crazier than hell, right?"

Ben chuckles. "The people from Queen Hill did seem different, somehow. When we were kids, anyway. But they really weren't."

"Right. So, the man parks the truck there in that leveled-off area, which curved around the bottom of the hill where the people used to park their cars, right? And we get off and he gives us the price of each item and says he'll pay us a nickel for every fifty cent's worth we sell. Hold on I say, reminding him that he had said a dime before. And he looked at Danny and me and removed the piece of straw he had in his mouth and said that a nickel plus a nickel makes a dime. Well, shit, I thought. But anyway, it's been a while since either Danny or I have seen a nickel, so we agree.

"So, the man says we are to do the hill in sections by working one trail at a time. Danny takes the houses to the left of the trail and I take the houses to the right. Right away Danny begins to make sales but every house I go to nobody wants to buy anything. So, Danny makes a sale, runs down to pick up whatever was purchased, delivers it, goes on to the next house, makes a sale, runs down, and on and on. And meanwhile I cannot make sale one.

"Anyway, I walk up to this house and knock on the door and this lady comes out to the porch and I say, *Señora, quiere comprar elote o chile verde o tomate?* 'WHAAAT?' the lady says. It seems to me that she is upset because I have spoken Spanish to her although she did look Mexican to me. I am sorry, I say, switching to English, would you like to buy some corn or green chile or tomatoes? Now, the lady is looking at me with eyes that are burning holes in me and she is getting redder and redder in the face as though she is just starting to come to grips with the outrageous fact that I have insulted her by speaking Spanish. Well, this old lady, whom I had never seen before, is standing there glaring at me and then the fingers on her hands begin to twitch. Obviously, looking back, I suppose she had some kind of affliction which caused her hands to twitch that way, you know, like some people do when they get old. But what I am thinking at the time is that those twitching fingers are a sign that she would like nothing better than to wrap her hands around my skinny, Spanish-speaking throat. Yeah, that's what I'm thinking. So, I take a couple of steps back just in case. I say to her, well? And she answers, well what? I take another step back and say, would you like to buy some corn or not? 'NO,' she yells, and turns around and slams her door hard.

"So, right off the bat I'm off to a bad start, Ben, and that throws me off quite a bit. I decide that the next house up I'll just wait until the person asks me what do you want or *que quiere* and that way I'll know how to respond. I don't want the same thing to happen again. So, I walk up to the next house and on to the front porch and knock and this lady comes to the door and looks at me and I look at her, waiting. We're just standing there looking at each other. She is waiting for me to say something and I am waiting for her to say something. What I'm thinking is that I don't want to see any more twitchy hands so what's it going to be lady, English or Spanish? Come on now, I don't have all day here. That's what I'm thinking. And she, well, she starts to get this puzzled look on her face. Which of course, looking back, I don't blame her. I mean, here is this kid who comes and knocks on her door and then just stands there looking at her. Give me a break. Well, I am still flustered about the first lady and confused, so out of my mouth pop the words, *what do you want?* You know what I'm saying here, Ben? I have knocked on her door, disturbed her nap or cooking or housecleaning or whatever she was doing, and I am asking *her* what *she* wants. 'GET OFF MY PORCH, YOU LITTLE SMART ALECK,' she yells at me.

"So off I go back out of her yard and on up the trail and I decide that this is a very inefficient way to do business. I think about it for a bit and come up with a plan. Instead of going house to house, I can just call out that there are vegetables for sale in both Spanish and English. That way the whole neighborhood can get the word and there won't be any trouble about it. I'm thinking that what better advertising can there be for your product than a kid yelling at the top of his lungs, right? Since Danny and I had already lost a nickel between the time we jumped on that old guy's truck and Queen Hill, I thought I had better speed things up. We were wasting time by going house to house and time is money as the saying goes. What I hadn't thought about was the fact that a lot of those old guys worked shift work and might be sleeping during the day.

"So, anyway, sure enough, no sooner did I start yelling when through the branches of a fig tree I see this girl come charging out of her porch and into her side yard. *'Oye tu, gritón,'* she called out to me, 'cut out that yelling. Don't you know that my father is asleep?' Well, the girl comes around the tree to take a look and her eyes

102

narrow as she recognizes me. 'IT'S *YOU!*' She yelled. Yeah, she recognizes me all right. It was Della Luna, and my heart skips a beat or two. This is not good, not good at all. There had been some kind of misunderstanding between us even before what happened that previous winter.

"On that day, after school, I was standing by that big furnace chimney. You know, the one there between the hotel and the company store which came up out of the concrete and where all us kids used to warm ourselves when it was cold. Well, I was standing there with my back up against the thick, warm metal when the Luna sisters, Stella and Della, came around the corner of the hotel walking real slow. You remember them, don't you, Ben?"

Ben hadn't thought of the Luna sisters for many years but then they pop up clearly into his mind. He is happy to remember them, a feeling he always gets when he remembers someone from childhood. He recalls that the sisters were very bright in school and also at times a bit different in their ways. "Yes, I remember them." Ben smiles, "They were a year or two older than we were, right?"

"Yeah, I think so. By the way, what ever happened to them?"

Ben thinks for a moment. "Well, it seems to me that they went on to college in California and graduated and married well. Doctors or lawyers I think, not sure. Later on, I heard they became active in political affairs out in the L.A. area."

"Is that right? Good for them. So, anyway, Stella was the older one and Della was the one who didn't like me for some reason and that was even before what happened that day. I was never quite sure why she disliked me, since I had never done anything to her."

Ben turns toward Sal and laughs. "Well, you probably did *something* to her, Sal."

"Maybe I did but I don't remember. Anyway, she was half-crazy, and she didn't like me. So, as I was saying, the snow had melted from the day before and all that concrete area was icy. Now, if you remember the concrete had a gradual slope to it, like a ramp, as it went down toward the back doors to the company store. A bunch of us kids had been fooling around there by sliding down on the ice toward the doors where we would stop our forward motion by extending our arms and catching ourselves up against the wall of the store. Sometimes we made it all the way without falling. But by then all the kids had left, and I was warming myself one last time before heading home when I see Stella and Della come walking around the walkway by the hotel. So, they are just approaching the ramp and walking very slow because of the ice when Della turns to Stella and says in a voice loud enough for me to hear. 'Oh, I can't stand that guy. He thinks he is so smart, warming himself there.' They take another couple of slow steps and then I walk up behind them. I decide to just go around them and slide on down to the doors. I was probably showing off. Well, just as I get to the bottom, I can see in the reflection of the glass portion of the doors that Della has slipped and fallen on the ice. And here she comes sliding down toward the doors with her legs way up in the air and picking up speed. I can see her panties and everything. Now I know that if she slams into the doors, she will probably hurt herself, especially in that position. I don't know what to do, Ben. I know I can't stop her momentum by myself. I think I probably weighed maybe eighty pounds at the time. And Della was a big girl, if you will recall. So, the only thing I can think of is to open the door and let her slide on by and come to a stop by herself inside the store. I think I'm doing a good thing. I mean, if you see someone hurtling down on a collision course with some obstacle and you can remove that obstacle you should do it, right? It will be my good deed for the day. I can tell Mr. Velasquez all about it. Maybe there's some kind of merit badge for things like that. That's what I'm thinking and that's what I do, and she goes by me and on into the store where she does not stop but keeps sliding along still in that same position. And then her momentum carries her onto the polished hardwood floor to the butcher shop area where she finally comes to a stop just before she hits a big stack of boxes of crackers that are on display.

"Well, there were several people in the area, men and women, and they are all startled of course but then they politely look away.

No one said anything. Stella comes in and helps her sister up to her feet and helps her to pull her coat and dress back down and Della dusts herself off and stomps away toward the stairs to the second and third floors but not before she gave me a look that had no thank you in it at all, and I had better not hang around there waiting for one. No sir. And just about every time after that whenever she saw me, she would give me that same look and say something under her breath and there were a couple of times she chased me half the way home. Needless to say, I gave her plenty of space.

"So, now, in her yard, she started looking around on the ground for a rock to throw at me. Well, she couldn't find one handy so instead she picked up a fig from beneath the fig tree in her yard and threw it at me. So, Ben, you and I both know that just about anything you throw at a kid, besides a rock, he will catch. It's just pure instinct, right? Well, I caught the fig she threw at me. You know, kind of cool and casual, no big deal. And then, having the fig in my hand, I figure what the heck and I start to eat it.

"Yes sir. That's what I did. God help me. And Della's reaction to that sight was to jump three feet up in the air and scream at the top of her lungs some words I couldn't quite make out except for the usual and popular *tu madre* here and there. And I could not blame her. Absolutely not. I mean, come on, when you throw something at someone in anger you don't want them catching it and eating it, for God's sake. It's just not right. What I should have done was duck and apologize like any right-thinking kid ought to do, right? But no, I ate the damn fig, of all things. And then, you know how some women's hair will kind of stand up when they're mad? Like there is some kind of electrical activity going on up there? Well, there it was, and Della started scrambling around her yard hissing like one pissed off cat. And again, I don't blame her for that either. I mean, how dare me? And then she did find a rock, about the size of a grapefruit, and she came flying out of the gate with another scream that made my advertising sound like a whisper. AAAAARG, she yelled. So, I lit out and she came chasing after me cursing and yelling for me to stop in both Spanish and English. And it was very clear that if she caught me there was going to be some serious ass-whipping taking place on that mountain, period.

"I was thinking she would tire out quickly, but I thought wrong, again, because it seemed to me that her anger was allowing her to gain on me, which scared me and then my legs kicked it into high gear. So, there we go up one trail and down the other but after a couple of loops she did tire out and went back home. Or so I thought.

"Well, I started to walk back down the trail and when I got close to the Luna's house, I switched over one trail and went back down that way. I was winded when I got back to the truck and the old guy asked me what the hell had been going on up there. I was fed up by then and I didn't care what he had seen so I told him that this girl had been following me trying to negotiate for a lower price on his corn. He frowned at me and asked what it was she had in her hand. Oh, I said, she had a handful of figs that she wanted to trade for some vegetables, but I told her that my boss dealt in cash, and cash only. The old guy had a disgusted look on his face and said, 'You had better improve your sales, boy. I'm trying to run a business here.' So, the old guy moves his truck forward a short distance to the shady side of the mountain next to that long row of tall oleanders which grew alongside the bottom of the hill. Where, by the way, Ben, some people said they had seen a ball of fire one night and everyone said it was a sign that there was a witch living in those bushes, if not the Devil himself. Anyway, the old guy gets out and tells me to watch the vegetables while he walks up one of the trails and disappears.

"So, I am standing by the truck trying to catch my breath and looking up the hill to see if I can catch a glimpse of Danny when I think I see Della coming down the trail and it looks to me like now she has a good-sized stick in her hands but then I lose sight of her behind the oleanders. I carefully consider my situation and it doesn't look good, Ben. Nope, not good at all. Number one, Della is half crazy to start with and that's a fact. Number two, I've got two strikes against me already. Namely, I have seen her panties and I ate her fig. So, I am in bad shape. Very bad shape, and I'm thinking that Della no longer cares whether her sleeping father wakes up or about any of her daughterly chores such as whether supper is cooking on the stove or whether the kitchen needs mopping or whether little junior needs his diaper changed. No sir, this girl has bigger fish to fry. And it is obvious to me what all this boils down to is that I have tipped her scales and put her over the edge. I have driven her insane. And since it is all my fault, I am thinking that the right thing to do is just let her come on out and whack me a couple of times with her stick and let her get it out of her system and be done with it. So, I wait to see at what point she will come charging out of the bushes. But nothing happens. And then I hear a rustling sound coming from that direction and out comes this mangy old dog, whimpering and carrying on, and then he runs away on down the road.

"Now, I had heard or read somewhere that dogs can smell fear, and I am wondering now if maybe they can smell hate also. I am looking intently into the bushes when Danny shows up. He says, 'What are you looking at, Sal?' I tell him that Della Luna is hiding in the bushes with a big stick and she wants to grab me and teach me a lesson. Danny says, 'Oh yeah? Whatever. I need a dozen ear of corn and six tomatoes.' And he looks at me, with a piece of straw sticking out of his mouth, like he is waiting for me to fill that order. I make no move so he just sort of shakes his head and starts to put those items into a paper sack himself. Danny, I say, didn't you hear what I just said? It's Della Luna and she might kill me, for God's sake. Danny stops putting the ears of corn into the paper sack and turns to me and says, 'Sal, if you can't sell you just can't sell. There's them that can and there's them that *cain't*.' That's how he said it, Ben. *Cain't*. I look at him and think, I'll be damned. And then he said, 'You don't need to be making up stories to get around it. Frank and I have a business to run here and we have decided that it is best if you just watch the truck.' And he finishes packing his order and trots off before I have a chance to laugh in his face.

"So, what we have here, Ben, is that Danny has sold a few

vegetables and he is suddenly a *businessman* and he is now talking just like the old man, with whom he is now on a first name basis by the way. And he and this so-called Frank have discussed the matter partner to partner, each with a piece of straw in his mouth, of course, and after much thought and careful consideration they have decided that it would be in the best interest of the company if I were demoted to truck watcher. So, in other words, I ain't shit. And to top it all off there's a crazy person lurking in the bushes who is no doubt carefully studying my position and otherwise planning all kinds of nonsense that involve her big stick and the top of my head.

"So now I am pissed off. I don't need this crap. I am thinking the hell with all those people who wouldn't buy any vegetables from me, the hell with that straw-chewing old man, the hell with Danny and, lastly, the hell with that crazy Della. And I am tempted to go into those bushes and tear that stick from Della's hands and show her what's what.

"Those are my thoughts when a man comes walking down the trail and approaches me. He is a tall, handsome, friendly looking guy. He smiles at me and says, '*Hola, joven. Que tal?*' *Todo bien,* I say. Then he says, 'Were you the guy that was yelling up there a while ago?' I'm thinking that this is my chance to get back at Danny-the-businessman, so I say, no sir, that was Danny, Danny Rios is his name and he lives up on Heaven Hill, in that blue house by the church. If you want to wait for him, he should be back down in a minute. 'No, no,' the man says, 'I've got to go. But be sure and thank him for me for waking me up. My daughters sometimes forget. *No hacen caso, pues.* I need to pick up a package at the post office before it closes.' So, the man gets into his car and starts it up and then turns it off and comes back to the truck where he buys fifty cents worth of corn and tomatoes and green chile and then he asks me if I can take them up to his house. Sure, I say, which one is it? He points up in the direction of a white house with gray trim. You're not talking about that one with a fig tree in the side, are you? 'That's the one,' he says then he adds, 'boy, you sure have good eyes.' So, I say, are you Della's father? He says he is and asks me if I know her. Yes, I do, I say, and she is in those bushes right over there. He looks over toward the bushes and laughs and tells me that I am mistaken because he had just left his house and Della was helping her mom fix dinner.

"So, it was all my imagination apparently, Ben, and she had not been in the bushes at all. And I might as well go on up to her house and deliver the corn and tomatoes and face the music. So up I go, happy that I've made a sale at last.

"I walk straight up onto the porch and knock on the door. Stella, the older sister, comes out of the door quickly and puts her hand behind my neck and walks me to the other end of the porch. 'You've got some nerve,' she says in a low voice, 'coming up here with a few measly vegetables, as though that will take care of everything.' It is obvious to me that she is not aware her father has paid for the vegetables. She thinks I have brought them up as a peace offering and I do not correct the misunderstanding. What do you mean? I ask. 'Don't act dumber than you look,' she says, 'you know Della wants to do some real bad things to you.' I am thinking that Stella appears to be the more reasonable of the two, and very good looking if you will recall, and that perhaps she and I can discuss the matter in a sensible manner. I ask her why Della hates me. 'Ha,' she says, 'as though you didn't know.' Well, I don't, I say. She says, 'Yeah, sure, like you didn't see her panties that day.' I didn't see her panties, I say. Stella looks at me. 'Were they torn?' She says this very softly as though it can be something strictly between the two of us. No, I say. She raises her voice. 'Aha,' she says, 'so you *did* see them.' No, I say, what I mean is that I didn't see any panties, torn or otherwise. I saw zero panties. She quickly reaches out and pinches my arm, not hard but not soft either. 'Be quiet, you silly little thing,' she says, and then she lowers her voice again. "And, I suppose you didn't eat that fig she threw at you either.' Well, I say, that I did do but only because I hadn't had any breakfast and I was very hungry, since selling vegetables is a lot of work. Stella gave me a hard look, studying me up and down, and then she says, 'Della says you always walk around all smart-alecky. Do you deny that too?' I had no idea what that meant, Ben, but I told her that if it would help matters, I was even willing to change my walk. Stella laughed at me. She looked like she was getting ready to pinch me again but instead cuffed me lightly on the top of my head. 'You really are just a total little liar, aren't you? I am beginning to see why Della can't stand you. She says you made that ice slippery on purpose just so she would slip and fall, and you could see her panties, you little *cochino*.' Please, Stella, I say, I don't want any trouble.

"Ha, she goes, cuffing me with one hand and pinching me with the other. She tells me I already have trouble, and lots of it, because the one person you really don't want to mess with in all of Queen Hill is Della Luna and everybody knows that except, she guesses, poor little dumb me. She was standing very close to me and I was thinking she had pretty eyes to go with her pretty face when her eyes start to move back and forth from one of my ears to the other. She reaches out and pulls one of them as though checking to see if it is fully attached. 'Where'd you get those ears? Wow. I'd like to get me a pair like that.' She flicks one of my earlobes back and forth. 'I could fly.' Please Stella, I say, for God's sake.

"She waited a bit, like she was thinking or getting bored with me and I thought she would let me go and I could just walk away but then she told me again how I had messed with the wrong person and she starts telling me what all Della wants to do to me. She tells me that at night when she and Della are in bed and Della can't sleep she will talk about how much she can't stand me for making that ice slippery and how she wants to rip off one of my ears and put it in a special big jar which she has already set aside for just that purpose, and that she has a label on the jar and that it says Rat Face Sal's Left Ear, and that she would like to someday just walk up to me and poke my nasty, panty-seeing eyes out, and also someday she wants to slap my face so hard that the blow will knock all my teeth out and then she wants to sit on my chest till I can't breathe and scratch her name on my forehead and then all the girls won't think I'm so great, what with me having only one ear and no teeth and her name scratched on my forehead.

"Hold it right there, Stella, I say, but she just keeps on going. Stella says, that Della says, that maybe my forehead is so tiny that she will only be able to get her first initial on there and maybe it will have to be a little *d* since my forehead probably can't accommodate a big *D* and maybe she will have to wait until my little rat face forehead and the rest of me gets bigger, like maybe when I am a senior in high school and so on and so forth.

"I don't know what to do, Ben. Is she serious? I speak up. Wait just a darn minute, I say, I don't have to stand here and listen to all of this stuff about rats and jars and ripped off ears and whatever. I have a job to do and I'm leaving. Stella waves her hand in front of my face as though she is shooing away a fly. 'Don't try to change the subject, Ratty. What you need to do is run down to that truck and bring us back two watermelons, one for me and one for Della and on Della's you need to write, To Della, with all my love. P. S. I did not see your panties that day. And then maybe everything will be all right, but I can't guarantee it. Who knows, maybe she'll choke you right away, maybe she won't, maybe here, maybe on the playground.' Well, then it dawns on me that Stella has been pulling my leg all along. She's just been messing with me. I start to laugh, and I am laughing away, ha, ha, ha, I go, that's a good one Stella, when Della comes out of the door and sees me and freezes, like a cat that's spotted a rat. 'Hold on, Della,' Stella says, 'Rat Tail here has explained everything to me and the reason he acts so stupid is because he has a terrible crush on you and he just can't help himself. And, he has brought you a bag of vegetables and he is just about to run down and get us a couple of watermelons to make up for all the trouble he's caused us, and he is going to write a special little message on yours. Isn't that right, Rat Nose?' Della relaxed then and sort of smiled at me and purred like a cat.

"The heck of it was that the old guy wasn't selling watermelons and that put a whole different spin on the situation. And no sooner did I mention this to the girls when there was a blur of activity on that porch which ended up with Della wrestling me to the floor and sitting on my chest in no time flat. I was trapped and desperate, so I just blurted out that I would take them both to the Saturday matinee in place of watermelons. The problem was that I had no idea where I would get the money to treat them to the movie. But when I got down to the bottom of the hill the truck was just starting to pull away and I ran alongside it to tell the old guy that I had made a sale and give him the fifty cents that Della's father had paid me. 'YOU'RE FIRED,' the old guy yelled at me, and left me in the dust.

"So, the next Saturday I met the girls in front of the theater, and I paid for the tickets and we went inside and sat down. I was sitting between them and it was dark and cool and just when the movie was starting to get good Della leaned over to me and asked me for the fourth time if I really, really, hadn't seen her panties that day. For God's sake, Della, I said, I did not. 'Well,' she whispered into my ear and placed her hand over mine, 'would you like to see them now?' Whoa, I said to myself. I don't know about this. Sure, I said, but first I need to go to the restroom, okay? So, I got up and excused myself and walked up the aisle and through the lobby and out of the theater and ran all the way home just to see how fast I could get there.

"I felt bad for Della, I really did, but also about missing the rest of that movie. It was a western with Randolph Scott. You know, bullets flying, dead cowboys all over the place. So, anyway, it seems to me now that I made up some story later about why I had to leave the theater that day. I waited until Della was with Stella and a group of their friends on the playground and I marched right up to her and told her the story and promised her that as soon as I saved up my money I would take her to the movies again but this time just the two of us. No one else allowed. Stella gave me a look like she might slap me right then and there just for the hell of it, but Della blushed and giggled and seemed okay with my plan. For three or four weeks she told everyone I was her boyfriend. Then she told them she had to break up with me because I was just too poor and never had any money for the movies."

Ben laughs, as he has all along at Sal's story. The small

communities at the outskirts of Farmsdale have now appeared, and he needs to use the restroom. "Sal, I need a stop."

"Okay. We need to fill up, and there's a gas station up ahead. But I thought we could wait to have breakfast at the old Charro in Stanton. Seems to me they had the best food back then." Sal pauses. "And now that I think about it, didn't you and China and Rita and I eat there after a prom way back then?"

Ben tries to recall that particular memory, but it evades him. Other memories rush in. "Yes...you're right, it was the best."

17

The men are silent as they drop down the long hill into the town of Stanton and cross the bridge over the sparkling river. In the narrow main street of the town by a steep canyon wall they arrive at the old restaurant.

"Damn, Ben. This used to be a lively place. Vacant buildings all up and down the street now."

"Yeah, Sal. When the mine shut down it had an impact here and even in Farmsdale back there."

"You lived down here for a while?"

Ben looks down the narrow street. All the businesses are boarded up. The union hall sign is faded and slants down. He thinks of the raucous meetings in that hall back then, followed by more of the same after they adjourned to the bar across the street. He dimly recalls a cold and rainy day during a long strike around Thanksgiving when from the doors of that union hall they were handing out food vouchers.

"Yes. I lived in a tiny apartment above that store over there." He remembers struggling up those dark, narrow stairs to a dark room and then looking out of the window down at the lights of the long narrow street of the town. When he thinks of those days and his state of mind back then it seems as though he is remembering another person, not himself. He draws away from the memory with effort and returns to the present.

There is a young couple and a little boy at a corner table in the restaurant. They smile at Ben and Sal. The place is still bright and clean, and the food still smells as good as it did back then. The owner, Soledad, now gone many years, always had a smile and words of encouragement for Ben and a discount on his bill. Ben had his last meal there on the day he left the area for California. He always thought he would see her again.

After breakfast at the restaurant Ben and Sal start the climb to Orenville. Three miles from the town a roadside sign reads, "Orenville. Private Property. The Dome Corporation." They continue up the steep road, past the smelter where a large sign hangs on a tall chain link fence gate that reads "Closed. Trespassers will be prosecuted." A thick chain with a huge lock secures the gate. The road rises higher still and then they go through the overpass where the trains used to run and then up to the narrow tunnel through the rock of the mountain and on to the curve by a wide empty place where the high school used to be and then on up to the plaza.

Sal's voice trembles as he speaks. "Good God, Ben."

There is not a house remaining in what was once a town of five thousand people. Here and there the men see a foundation or a retaining wall or steps leading nowhere. The two remaining intact mountains of Orenville stand as barren reminders of what once was. Half of Heaven Hill is gone. In its place now there is blue sky. Sal gasps and then curses. The front wall of the theater and one tall, jagged portion of the company store are all that remain as reminders of the plaza. There is a wide, dusty swath through the center of the town that rises gradually and disappears in the direction of the mine entrance where there is another gated chain link fence.

Sal parks the car in the wide space that used to be the plaza. The men are silent as they struggle with the image before then. Each man tries to find a point of reference to visualize the high school, the grade schools, the hotel, the club where they had their graduation dance, the ivy covered fence of the park where the tall pines grew and young lovers loitered on Sunday afternoons, the fish pond, the wishing well, and then on to the steps by the theater leading up to the shopping center with its market, jewelry store, clothing store, five and dime store, furniture store, post office, restaurant, drug store, barber shop, beauty shop, and dentist office.

Ben and Sal look further up the hill at the empty spaces that used to be the bar and restaurant, the church in which they were married, the bakery, hardware store, herb store, shoe repair shop, grocery stores, and then on another hill the hospital where they were born. They look up at the hundreds of empty spaces of the houses and the trails that ran between them. Each house a home. As Ben tries to fill in all that is gone, memories spring up of walking along all the old roads and trails. He recalls the gradually rising portion of the path below the church, the houses along the way, the herb store with the large front window, the lumber yard, the ally approaching home. Briefly, faintly, and then clearly comes the smell of food. Each smell rising distinct and separate—bacon, tortillas cooking on stoves, potatoes, eggs, chorizo, beans bubbling on a skillet, red chile sauce simmering, rice browning, pasta toasting, green chile roasting, and meatloaf, and coffee, and a cake baking, and somehow coming through it all the smell of home brew—then all them blending together and gone.

Sal walks away in the direction of the company store while Ben moves in the opposite direction and looks out toward the south where the break in the mountains of Orenville presents an unobstructed view of the high desert hills rolling away as far as the eye can see. The crisp breeze makes his eyes water. Ben turns back and looks at the blank marquee of the theater. He looks at it for a moment or two, trying to remember the name of a movie. After he gives up, the name comes in a whisper. *"Brigadoon."*

Ben and China walked down to the theater at dusk. It was cold and it felt like it might snow and all along the steps and paths that led down to the plaza they met smiling people coming up laden with bags of groceries from the company store. Inside the theater, while they were watching Gene Kelly and Cyd Charisse on the screen, someone in a row behind them said that it had started to snow.

The movie fascinated Ben. It was the story about a village that came into existence on just one day every hundred years. While the inhabitants of that village and Cyd Charisse would age one day, the outside world along with Gene Kelly would age one hundred years. Two different dimensions of time. One fast, one slow.

When Ben and China walked out of the theater there were large snowflakes floating down on top of the inch or two of snow already on the ground. The wide parking lot between the theater and the company store was deserted so that a pure whiteness lay before them. China removed her cloth gloves and a silver silk scarf from the pockets of her new green coat and put them on before stepping out from the portico of the theater. They walked across the parking lot and climbed the steps that led up to the hotel. It was from those steps that the high school band would play Christmas carols on Christmas Eve while the men from the American Legion, one of them dressed up as Santa Claus, would hand out the bags of fruit and nuts and candy to the children. Ben and China stood arm in arm and looked across the street at the Christmas lights on the tall pine trees in the plaza.

"Ben, that village existed for just one day every hundred years?"

"Yes." Ben looked at China's profile in the glow of the Christmas lights. As he studied her face, a snowflake landed on her eyelash and made it flutter. China laughed and wiped it away. Ben turned and looked up at the lights of the houses on Heaven Hill. He could see Christmas lights in the windows. He looked for his own house but could not quite make it out.

"Did you like the movie?"

"Yes, China, and you?"

China was quiet for a moment. She also looked up at Heaven Hill. "Yes, but sad." She wiped at her eyes again. "Do you think Orenville will one day be gone?"

Ben laughed. "Do you mean like Brigadoon?"

"I mean, do you think that one day the mine will run out of copper?"

"Yes, probably. Nothing lasts forever."

China pressed up closer to Ben, nudging him. "I think love does."

They walked back toward the theater and then around it to the steps that led up to the shopping center. Without turning toward Ben, China said, "Ben, Sal told Rita that they call you 'Mad Dog Medina.'"

Ben laughed. "It's just a name, China. It doesn't mean anything. Sergeant Pittman just made it up, you know, to create interest. He has names for all the boxers on the team."

"That's all?"

"Yes. And I'll only do it a little while longer, until my enlistment is up."

They walked around the side of the shopping center and then up the steps by the two-story company general office building and then on to the road that went up to Heaven Hill. When they got to the steps in front of the church, they turned to look back down at the center of the town. It looked distant and fragile and peaceful, and there was a soft blue color to it. They entered the church and sat for a few minutes in a pew by the flickering glow of the votive candles in their many-colored glass jars. Outside again, they continued up the winding path, stopping once in a while to kiss and look back at their footprints in the snow.

From inside Ben's house came the sound of laughter and music as he and China walked up the front steps and onto the porch. It was warm inside and there was the aroma of tamales steaming on the stove and the smell of the fresh pine tree that Ben's father had brought down from the mountains behind the town. There were brightly wrapped presents beneath the tree and bowls of candy on the coffee table. There were three or four couples there, some of them just leaving, and all of them very well dressed as usual. The long-time friends were sharing a drink, a hot toddy concoction made with rum that Ben's father always made at Christmas time.

Later, after they'd eaten, Ben and China walked the rest of the way up Heaven Hill to China's house where there was a full-fledged party going on. The snow had stopped, and the stars were shining in the deep blackness of the sky and it was very cold. Outside, the men tended a fire under the high roof of an open-sided shed from which hung a low-watt light bulb. China's family cooked their tamales in the old way, in a large pot on a low cast-iron grill off to one side of the fire under which the men would add coals as needed. A few feet away from the shed some of the boys were playing their guitars and singing softly, going over the words of an old song.

China squeezed Ben's hand and walked into the house to be with the women while Ben remained outside with the men by the fire. Each man greeted and embraced him. Some of the younger men were laughing and taking turns telling stories about each other. A bottle of brandy came around and as Ben lifted his head to drink from it a shooting star moved brightly across the Milky Way. From inside the house the sound of the laughter of the women rose and rippled out into the chill of the night. Ben felt the warmth of the fire and the warmth of the brandy going down.

Two of the older women came out of the house and briefly exchanged banter with the older men. Laughing at their responses, one of the men lifted the large lid of the pot exposing the white cloth covering the tamales. It was as white as the snow. A big puff of steam rose up when one of the women folded the cloth back. She held a large copper platter with handles on it while the other woman filled it with layers of tamales and then covered them with another white cloth. They told the men everything was ready, time to come in and eat.

The bottle came around again. Ben looked at the fire and then out at the town to the lights on the other hills down to the Christmas lights of the plaza far below. The air grew colder as the men began to move toward the house. Ben fell in behind them as the sound of laughter once again came across the snow.

Ben looks up once again at the remains of Heaven Hill. He walks back to the car, lights a cigarette, and sits on the front bumper looking down at the ground. Sal walks back to join him and reaches over to remove the pack of cigarettes from Ben's jacket pocket. He takes out a cigarette and lights it. Neither man speaks until they have finished their cigarettes.

"Are we ready, Ben?"

Ben looks at the high berm across the swath that prevents any vehicle from going up the hill. Ben thinks he should walk up, but it seems very far to him. He wonders how, as a boy, he had been able to run up the mountain for lunch and then back down to school.

Sal speaks again. "I had forgotten how blue the sky is here, Ben."

"So blue it hurts your eyes?" Ben looks at Sal.

"Yeah," Sal answers, as he rubs his eyes. He takes out his handkerchief and blows his nose.

They get back into the car and turn around and go back down to the entrance to the town where a separate road climbs up behind Queen Hill.

The old cemetery rises steeply from the dirt road. Here and there, through the prickly pear cactus and yucca are newly painted silver metal fences around some of the graves but mostly the fences are of very old and deteriorated wood. Some of the graves have only a cross made of pipe or lopsided wooden crosses held together with wire. Some of the bare spaces have only a few pieces or splinters of wood where a cross used to be. Ben remembers the sound of the picks and shovels scraping against the rock and the sound of the grunting of the men as they dug the graves. There were times when the men would come across very hard rock and they would have to use dynamite. Further around the curve of the hill are the newer graves. Ben and Sal find the trail and walk in that direction. Somewhere up ahead there is the soft beating of the wings of a covey of quail as they fly away.

Sal looks at Ben and asks a question with his eyes. "Over there," Ben says, pointing out Sal's grandmother's grave. Sal moves away to the left and begins to climb the trail. Ben turns to the right and counts three graves up and five to the right. He approaches China's grave. He places his hand on the headstone and holds it there for a few moments with his eyes closed. Then he kneels and begins to remove the small, tough clumps of dry wild grass from the inside edges of the curb of the grave.

O n a bright morning in May, Ben and Sal waited on the shady side of the church sharply dressed in their military uniforms when the altar boy came out and told them it was time. They checked each other out one final time for proper appearance and bearing—all lines crisp and clean, shoes shined, ties snug and correctly tucked. Satisfied, they shook hands and walked in and up to the altar where the rest of the wedding party was in place and waiting. The organ began playing and Mr. Villa came down the aisle with two visions of loveliness, Rita on one arm and China on the other. Twins, but different, each had her own special beauty and their radiant smiles filled the packed church. The reception and dance were at the Minero Dancehall. Leading the wedding march at two o'clock in the afternoon were the two oldest residents of the town, Doña Pilar and Don Albino. The line of couples joining the march stretched out of the dancehall into the road.

At the end of his enlistment Ben returned to Orenville where he and China settled into the day to day life of marriage. The seasons moved by with love and laughter and Sara was born. Then came the day of the accident and suddenly Rita was gone. China's occasional headaches, mild at first, became more frequent and troublesome but at the hospital they could find nothing wrong. Then, one morning in the spring, Ben came home from working the night shift and China had breakfast waiting for him as usual and drank her coffee and sat with him as he ate. Little Sara toddled into the kitchen with sleepy eyes and tousled hair. She came and sat in the chair next to Ben. From her own cup China poured a dash of coffee into a tiny porcelain cup and added cream and sugar and placed it in front of Sara who drank it daintily. Ben and China smiled at their daughter and sat and talked and listened to the singing of the birds in the trees in their front yard. Ben was saying something to China when a puzzled look came over her face and she said, "Oh." And then again, "Oh, Ben." She lowered her head to her folded arms and then she was gone.

Ben hears the sound of Sal's voice. He has moved to Rita's grave and is cursing as he pulls the wild grass from her grave. He is cursing in both Spanish and English. Ben smiles. He himself would never think of using profanity in a cemetery, but Sal's cursing now gives him pleasure.

Sal calls up to Ben. "Are there any of the old timers left, Ben?"

"I guess, maybe one or two."

"How about those of our generation?"

"Maybe a few down in the new town but most of them moved away years ago. You know, during that long strike."

"So, there is nothing left of the Orenville we knew?"

Ben doesn't answer. He is thinking of Polito Gomez. His headstone is visible to him through an unpainted wood picket fence a few graves down. Polito was his friend and classmate. He died of pneumonia when he was ten years old.

Ben recalls the day began as a pretty spring morning but in the afternoon the wind sprang up and the sky turned yellow and the temperature began to fall. The wind carried the priest's invocations in and out of Ben's hearing. For some reason they opened the casket one last time and he saw the color of death on the puffy and almost unrecognizable face of his friend. It was after dark and cold when Ben got back home. He skipped supper and went to bed early. He listened to the gusting wind blowing late into the night until it finally quieted, then he slept.

Ben comes aware that Sal is standing over him. "Is Danny by here?" Sal asks. Ben stands up and leads Sal to a well-maintained grave with a small American flag placed in a holder embedded into the concrete curb. In that same area there are many other graves with flags.

"They finally found him?" Sal asks.

Ben is not sure of the year but as he begins to speak it comes. "Yes, his remains, they said. In 1978. But I don't know what they actually found. The coffin was very light."

Sal looks at the headstone. He speaks softly. "Well, here you are, Danny boy."

After a few moments Ben and Sal move away and walk separately among the graves. Ben can hear Sal's exclamations as he comes upon someone's grave. The two men gradually work their way back down to the road below the cemetery. They climb in the car and move slowly along the dirt road, back the way they'd come.

"I would like to take one last picture here, Sal," Ben says. *One last picture to complete my book.* Ben asks Sal to stand a few feet away so that he can catch Sal and the cemetery and the town.

Ben moves his camera until he has half earth and half sky. In the viewfinder Ben sees the picture. There is a single small white cloud in a sky of the deepest blue. In the brilliant sunlight, Sal squints slightly toward the camera. Behind Sal and down to the town are the partial walls of the company store and the theater and beyond that the remains of Heaven Hill. To Sal's side and slightly above him is the outline of the cemetery where an old tilted cross meets the sky.

19

"Sal, tell me a story…anything, about the old town."

The car speeds along once again on the open highway. The men have not spoken for almost an hour.

"Well, not sure about a story, Ben, but I saw Joe Vela's grave up there. I was thinking about him."

"He's there." Ben looks over at Sal. "They say he carried two wounded men out of harm's way. Died going for the third."

"Yes, I know. But I was thinking about how the teachers would tell us that we could be anything we wanted to be. And, well, to be honest, it seemed like those words were for some of the class but not for all."

"The Air Force Academy deal?"

"Right. Poor Joe. He believed the teachers. His dream was that he wanted to go to the academy and become a jet pilot. He asked the teachers how he should prepare for it, you know, which classes to take and all that. They encouraged some to prepare for college, but others not so much. Sometimes, when he brought it up in class, it didn't seem as though the teachers took him seriously. I've always wondered how that could be. Maybe some thought it was farfetched. He was a plain guy but that was his dream. An average guy, I guess, but not dumb."

"No, not dumb at all." Ben looks out of the side window and softens his voice. "Brave as hell, though." He thinks about Joe and how on the walls of his tiny bedroom there were photographs and excellent hand-drawn pictures of all kinds of airplanes. That was Joe's dream, flying fast and high into the wild blue yonder. And then, in the mud of a jungle of a land far away.... Ben clears his throat and waits a while. "Tell me something else about Orenville."

Sal hears the change in Ben's voice. "Sure, Ben, let me think." Sal lights a cigarette, cracks the window and hands the pack to Ben who lights his own. After a minute or so Sal says, "Do you remember Jane Jewel?"

The image of the lady in question comes to Ben's mind. Lady Jane, she was called. She lived alone in a stone house at the bottom of Heaven Hill. Some people said she was from New York and that she'd moved to Orenville back in the early Thirties when the mine had been shut down. Sometimes a man would come and stay with her for a week or two and then leave again. She was kind but also peculiar and there were lots of stories about her.

"Yes, I remember Lady Jane, Sal."

"Right, Lady Jane. So, anyway, one day my mother handed me four dollars and fifty cents and sent me down to the company store to see if I could get a five-dollar book from Don Beto. If you'll recall, the company issued those books redeemable at the store, with the detachable denominations inside and then charged the account of the worker. Come payday the amount was deducted from his paycheck. It was a vicious cycle for some people, no doubt. There were some men who got no check, just the stub showing the deductions for the books. You remember how there was always someone who needed cash for one reason or another and would sell a five-dollar book for four dollars. There were also ten-dollar and twenty-dollar books, and now that I think about it, those books would probably be called scrip. And, if you will also recall, the man who had the corner on that business was Don Beto who handled those transactions out of his car, which was always parked in front of the company store. He had a wooden leg, you know. He'd lost a leg in a mining accident. So that's how he made his living. He would pay four dollars for a five-dollar book and then sell it for four-fifty. He would also lend money. Do you remember all that, Ben?"

"Yes, I remember Don Beto very clearly. He lived on Crown Hill. I also remember some of the men who only got check stubs on payday. There was this look in their eyes...."

"I can imagine. So, anyway, I'm running down to the store and when I start to get close I reach in my pocket to check on the money and damned if the two quarters didn't manage to slip out of a small hole in my pocket somewhere along the way. I run back up the hill, but I can't find them. I'm in a hell of a predicament, Ben. There's no way I can go back to mother and say I've lost the money. She won't believe me. I've been to that well too many times. I sit down and think it out and what I come up with is that if Don Beto can buy a five-dollar book for four bucks, why can't I? I mean, what's the big deal? So, I start to hang around the store, but on the opposite side of where he parked his car. I ask a few people if they would like four dollars cash for a five-dollar book. They just laugh at me. And pretty soon Old Lady Jane comes by and I ask her, Miss Jane, would you like four dollars cash for a five-dollar book? And she looks at me for a few seconds and doesn't say anything. I get the impression she's not aware this is the going rate for a five-dollar book. I think she thinks I am pulling her leg or something. Then she says, 'Does Don Beto know what you're doing?' Sure, I say, I'm working for him. Well, quick as a wink she's got me by the elbow and hauls me around to the front of the store and up to Don Beto's car where there are a few men carrying on their business with him. She says, 'This boy says he is working for you. Is that true?' Well, they carry on a discussion for a bit and then Old Lady Jane lets go of me and walks in the store. Don Beto looks at me and asks me what's going on. I tell him how I lost part of the money and all that and he takes pity on me and says that he'll let me have a book for four dollars, but I have to work off the fifty cents. I agree, of course. He tells me he forgot his lunch that morning and that I am to run up to his house and get it and bring it back down to him. And, he adds, in the next day or so I am to clean up his back yard

126

and also that I am to be available as his messenger whenever he needs me. Okay, I say.

"Well, away I go and run up to Don Beto's house and pick up his lunch from his wife. On the way back down, I stop to rest there by that big house by the old hospital where the ivy grew so thick over the retaining wall between the houses that it formed a sort of cave. It was very cool in there, if you remember. Well, I am in there cooling off when I see Old Lady Jane coming up the long flight of stairs that ran all the way from the old hospital down to the Blue Bell Bar. She gets up to the landing that leads to where I am resting and just stands there for a minute. Then she turns and starts to walk towards that ivy cave. I'm scared. I don't want her to see me, so I wiggle back deep into the vines and hide. She walks in and I hold my breath. She reaches in her purse and pulls out a piece of paper and then she removes one of the smaller rocks up high in the retaining wall and takes out another piece of paper from there and places her piece of paper in that niche and replaces the rock. She walks back out and on up the steps. After I see her disappear out of view I come out of my hiding place and I get a toe hold and pull myself up to remove the rock and take out the piece of paper the old lady had placed there. It is like a half sheet of paper and it is wrapped around some money. There are three one-dollar bills. My heart starts beating fast. There are some numbers written on the paper. The numbers are written large and they are, well, looking back, it seems they were something like 217, 218, and 317. I put the paper and the money back and I scoot out of there and down to the plaza to take Don Beto his lunch."

Ben turns in his seat. He is suddenly very alert. "You've never told me that story before, Sal."

Sal looks over at Ben. "No, Ben, I don't think I ever told anybody. It just seemed so strange to me, and kind of scary. And after a while I tried not to think about it. But off and on over the years it has come back to me and it did again up there in the cemetery when I saw some of the dates on those graves."

Ben lights a cigarette. He feels as though his hands are shaking but when he looks at them, they are steady. He concentrates on Lady Jane, trying to remember everything about her. *Lady Jane Jewel*. The friend of the Mexicans of Heaven Hill. Always walking around and dropping in. Dressing weird. Acting odd. Ben takes a deep puff of smoke and exhales slowly.

"Do we have anything to drink, Sal?"

"I think there is a half-pint in the glove compartment, Ben."

Ben takes a drink. He offers the bottle to Sal who holds it for a moment without drinking from it and then hands it back. Ben's mind races. Old feelings resurface.

Somewhere, in some old book, he'd read that the company began employing undercover agents since the strike of 1903. That strike had been about the difference in pay between Anglo and Mexican workers. Ben wonders at the fact that in his youth there were still people on Heaven Hill who spoke of the company only in whispers.

Ben shudders. A memory comes to him of a windy November night. He'd gone down the hill to trade comic books with one of his friends. He was walking up the trail on his way back home when he saw one of the watchman's trucks coming along the straight part of the road down near the bottom of the hill. Not wanting to be seen by the watchman, Ben waited along the retaining wall beneath the road. The truck came to a stop directly above him in the darkness between two widely spaced light posts. Ben heard the door open and the voice of the watchman. "Tell him they need it by Friday." There was no answer and then the truck door slammed shut. The truck started up again and moved slowly away. When Ben peeked up over the wall, he saw a figure pass across the tail lights of the truck and then disappear into the darkness. He wonders now if that may have been Lady Jane.

"Sal, do you think maybe the older people were right? You know, about spies."

"I don't know, Ben, but I'm sure no one could ever suspect Old Lady Jane. And, even if she had been discovered, the company could have had any number of people make signed statements that the old lady was just plain crazy. Her cover could have been that she was supposed to be crazy."

"But who do you think the other person was, Sal? The person she left the money for?"

"Who knows? I'd rather not think about such things."

Ben is still holding the bottle. He opens the cap and takes another sip. He offers the bottle to Sal but Sal waves him off.

Ben's face is flushed as he turns toward Sal. "Those were house numbers, right?"

"I don't know what those numbers meant, Ben."

Ben remembers the meetings at his house. It would be late at night and several men would come over and discuss union business. The meetings stopped for a few months after his uncle and Sal's father were fired and banished.

"Sal, did you ever at the time try to match up those numbers?"

"No. I didn't want to know. But the numbers were written strange. Like diagonally, so I wasn't sure."

"Do you know whose house was 317?" Ben asks.

"Not really but I guess it would be up around the fork in the road there by Don Albino's."

"Isn't that where Chano Flores lived, in that area?"

"Could be, not sure, Ben."

"He was heavily involved in the union back then, wasn't he?"

"Not sure about that either. But I do remember he very suddenly just up and quit."

Ben takes another drink. "When you saw Lady Jane leave that note was it before or after your dad was fired?"

"I think it was after, Ben. I'm trying to think."

"I can't believe anyone up there would be an informant."

Sal laughs. "Well, Ben, the trick to being an informant is to not act like one."

"Still, Sal...hell, I don't know."

"Me neither, but I do know that when I came back from the Army the first time, I bought that old Plymouth and drove it for awhile until I could buy something new. Well, when I went to see

Phil Phelps, you remember him, worked for the company and sold insurance on the side, to get insurance for my new car, which was required by the bank before they would finance the deal, he kind of put me off and said that he would call me later with my rates. Well, I waited a few days and he didn't call and I'm thinking what's going on? Isn't this guy in the business to make money? So finally, I call him. He said he couldn't insure me. Why? I asked. Because, he said, the report came back that I was a reckless driver. What report? I asked. I've never had a ticket in my life, I said. I tried to get him to tell me who had given him that bullshit report. But he just said that he couldn't insure me and that was that. Anyway, I had to go down to Stanton and buy insurance with an agent down there who charged me twice the rate. I got screwed. So, the bottom line was that not only did the company control what time you went to work, what time you got off, where you lived and how you lived, it seems they had a say in how much you had to pay for car insurance. Damn it to hell. They controlled the housing, the schools, the utilities, the hospital, the theater, all the way down to how much you paid for groceries."

Ben looks at Sal and laughs. "I didn't mean to get you started, Sal."

Sal laughs also. "We're getting close to home, Ben. Let me have a damn drink."

They have made good time and are now on the descent into the valley. Ben looks down toward the sprawling city. The weather is very clear. The city stretches away until it fades into the horizon in the late afternoon sunlight. Sal takes a sip and holds the bottle in his hand. He smacks his lips and makes a rumbling sound in his throat. "You should have sued those bastards for twenty million, Ben." Sal taps the brakes to kick the car out of cruise control. He hands the bottle back and looks at Ben. "I wonder if there is a statute of limitations for assholery. You know like forgery, battery...assholery."

Ben gives a small laugh and looks away. A single idea has begun to seep into his thoughts. Old Lady Jane...eccentric, outlandish Lady Jane. Dim memories begin to flash and fade. Dusk. An old woman. An old woman dressed in black hurrying from house to house....

20

Ben sits in his living room and waits for Cindy to finish making his bed and tidying up. He hears the sound of her voice, but he is not sure what she is saying. His thoughts are centered on Sal's story. The incident has remained on his mind since the trip back from Orenville.

Cindy is a trained care giver, or aide as they are called. She sets out Ben's daily regimen of medications and scolds him when he misses any. Her duties include housekeeping and cleaning Ben's apartment once a week. She has been working at the Rose Garden for five years.

Cindy married her high school boy friend a week after graduation, a marriage very much against her father's wishes. It caused a rift that try as she might she had never been able to repair. The marriage lasted two years. A month after her husband walked out the door Cindy moved from Nebraska to the valley and started working at the Rose Garden where she met Ben and liked him right away. She saw kindness in his eyes. She thought the small scar, an inch or so long on his upper right cheek, somehow added to his good looks. As time went on, on those days when she saw that Ben was especially quiet and distant, she would flirt with him in a light-hearted way, but he never seemed to notice.

Now, as she comes out of the bedroom, Ben shifts away from Sal's story and tries to catch what she is talking about. "...and I said to Miss Judy, well now, what are we going to do about that?

And she didn't say a word back to me. She just looked at me like, well, like I wasn't there. You know how she gets sometimes, Mr. Medina?"

"Yes... I do." Ben leaves Orenville and Lady Jane and comes back fully to the present.

"Mr. Medina, do you think that she might be ready to go across the orchard?"

"I don't know, Cindy. Judy seems okay. Maybe she's just got things on her mind."

"What kinds of things, Mr. Medina?" Cindy looks at Ben expectantly, waiting for his answer. He looks at her. In that moment it suddenly dawns on him that this young lady has been making his bed and tidying up his apartment and putting out his medication for years and he has never asked about her last name or if she is married or if she has children or where she is from. He knows nothing about her.

"Cindy?"

"Yes, Mr. Medina."

"Would you mind telling me your last name?"

Cindy laughs. "Well of course not Mr. Medina. It is Vale."

"Are you married?"

"Divorced."

"You must have gotten married very young. Do you have children?"

"Yes, I got married a week after high school. And yes, I have a daughter. Her name is Emily. She's seven."

"And her father?"

"He left. Said he had to find himself and all that stuff."

"Does he keep in touch?"

"No, we haven't heard from him in years." Cindy smiles.

"I'm sorry."

"Oh, it's all right. We get along just fine."

It strikes Ben that in all those years this young woman has struggled and never said a word. Always a smile, always concerned about him. Yet, to him she is a mystery. He looks closely at Cindy.

She is standing by the door, ready to leave. "So, what things?"

"Well, I don't know. Maybe she is thinking about her life."

Cindy brings her hand up to her soft-brown hair and brushes it away from her eyes. "Yes, I suppose you're right, Mr. Medina. Miss Judy could be thinking about that." She opens the door, pauses for a moment, and then steps out. Through the window Ben sees her begin to walk away and then she comes back and opens the door again. "By the way, Mr. Medina. How was your trip?"

"Good, it was a good trip."

"What is the name of the town again?"

"Orenville."

"Is that it?" She indicates the framed photograph on the wall. Ben looks up at the picture. "Yes, that is Orenville." Ben pauses. "As it used to be. It is no longer there."

"What happened to it, Mr. Medina?" Ben smiles at Cindy. Her eyes, as usual, light up when she asks a question. As though she is truly interested in what the response will be. "Well, the mine kept expanding and everyone had to move."

"Just move away? Where to?"

"Further down the mountain. They built another town further down the mountain."

"It looks like it was an interesting place. All those houses packed so close together."

Ben stands up and walks over to the picture and puts his finger on a particular house. "That is where I lived, Cindy. When I was a boy I could step across our front yard and directly onto the roof of the two-story house below us. There was a tall mulberry tree in the front yard where in the summer I could pick the mulberries from the roof of that house." Ben laughs out loud at the memory and the times his mother scolded him for staining his clothes with mulberry juice which, she said, was very hard if not impossible to wash out.

Cindy walks into the apartment and up close to the photograph and stands next to Ben. Still looking at the photograph, she says, "You have a nice laugh, Mr. Medina. I don't think I've ever heard you laugh."

Ben glances at Cindy and laughs again. His laughter comes easily, which surprises him. He sees that she wears no make-up and the blush on her face has spread to the smooth, flawless skin of her neck. Around her neck is a thin, gold chain and attached to the chain is a gold pendant that looks like a Chinese symbol. "Please, Cindy, would you like to have a seat?" Ben is not sure why he has said this. He wonders at the appropriateness of his hospitality. Cindy smiles. "I would love to, Mr. Medina." She walks over and sits down on the couch with not a hint of self-consciousness or shyness. She is not shy, thinks Ben, yet she blushes easily. He wonders why that is so.

Ben sits down at the other end of the couch. "I'm sorry, do you have time? If you have other apartments to do, you may—"

"Yes, I have time, Mr. Medina."

Ben looks away for a moment, and then back at Cindy. "I notice your necklace. What is it?"

Cindy places her hand on the pendant and smiles, showing perfect teeth. "Oh, Emily gave this to me. She says it's a Chinese symbol for hope. When she gave it to me, she said that I should hope for a handsome prince. Then the next day she said it didn't matter if it was a prince at all and that I didn't have to hope for one. A couple of days after that she said that he didn't have to be handsome either just as long as he wasn't messy. She's a character, Mr. Medina."

"Emily is a pretty name. But, please, call me Ben. After all..."

Cindy smiles and says, "Ben it is, then."

Ben laughs at the quickness of her response. "When I was a boy, I was walking along that path there," Ben waves in the direction of the picture, "and I came upon an old Chinese coin imbedded in the clay of the path. I'd walked along that path many times but never seen it till then. I took it home and cleaned it up to a shine with some scouring powder. It had, as I later saw in other Chinese coins, a square hole in the middle. It seems to me I knew why they had that hole, but I have forgotten now."

Cindy has never heard Ben address her in this manner, in such a familiar and friendly manner. In her mind, she is drawn to the image of Ben as a young boy. Cindy speaks, hoping she is correct. "I...Ben," she clears her throat, "I think I read somewhere that it was for threading a string through them."

"Yes, maybe you're right." Ben thinks for a moment. He seems to remember some other reason, but it eludes him. "I was interested in that coin. It made me wonder. I thought about the man who may have lost that coin on his way to work. You see, back in the early days of the mine there in Orenville they had brought in quite a few Chinese men from San Francisco. They had a community of Chinese in Orenville back in the early days. At that time the work was all underground. One day there was a cave-in and it was said that quite a few of those men were trapped and their bodies never recovered. There was a cave back behind Heaven Hill..."

"Heaven Hill?" Cindy looks at Ben.

"Yes, the hill on which we lived in Orenville was called Heaven Hill."

"Hmmm..." Cindy smooths the skirt of her green and tan striped uniform over her knees and looks once again at the picture on the wall.

"We used to go into that cave, which was actually a long tunnel curving downward, and explore it as kids. The entrance was barricaded by rails, but we could slip through fairly easily. The walls and ceiling, here and there, of the tunnel were reinforced with old timber. One day we tried to see how far into the tunnel we could go with candles, but it was too scary. The darkness seemed to swallow up the light of our candles, so we did not venture in too deep. The next time we borrowed our fathers' lanterns and we could go in all the way to where the tunnel was partially blocked by a smaller cave-in that we could squeeze over and then on to another cave-in that was solid from top to bottom. The people said that behind that part of the mine was where the Chinese men had been trapped. I remember thinking of all those men who had probably brushed up against those timbers down there in the dark on their way in and out of the mine. It was spooky in there, thinking about men being trapped and all. And one of my friends, Danny Rios, who was killed in Viet Nam back before it became a war, said in a scary voice, *'one hundred skeletons'*. Just about that time they blasted at the open pit mine. Whenever they blasted at the mine, which was usually every day around three o'clock, the vibration of the explosion could be felt throughout the whole town. Now, the vibration of the explosion inside the tunnel was magnified. Dust fell from the ceiling. Needless to say, we boys were tripping over each other to get out of there. We never went back." Ben looks over at Cindy. She is sitting perfectly straight, but her upper body is turned slightly toward him. Ben moves over to his recliner so that he and Cindy may face each other.

"So, anyway, on the day I found the Chinese coin I was thinking about the man who had lost it. And I was thinking, as boys do, that maybe the man who had lost that coin was on his way to the mine that morning. On the morning of the cave-in that is. And I was thinking that the coin I held in my hand was the last thing he touched, that remained outside, after his death."

Cindy listens to Ben's words and the pleasant sound of his voice. Ben has stopped talking and is looking at her. She feels that she should say something. Her mind races. She wants to say something appropriate, something that will encourage Ben to say more. She raises her hand to her necklace and lets her fingers stroke at the pendant. "Well, M...Ben, I, gee..."

Ben laughs. He perceives her difficulty. "You are a good listener, Cindy. I appreciate your company." Ben waits. "I think I'll have a soda. Would you like one?"

Cindy is relieved. She laughs also. "Yes, thank you. I can get them." She begins to rise.

"No, Cindy. You are my guest. Please sit."

Ben returns from the kitchen with the soft drinks. He has poured the beverage over ice cubes in two tall, slender glasses. In the one for Cindy he has placed a straw.

"So, when I grew up and came back from the Army, I went to work for the company. For the first three years I worked at the crusher where sometimes pieces of wood of various sizes would come down along with the ore itself. We had to remove those pieces of old timber because it would interfere with the milling process down the line. That wood, of course, was from the various old mine shafts that were continually being exposed as the open pit mine kept growing." Ben pauses and takes a sip of the soft drink. "There were times, depending on the location of the mine from which the ore was being hauled, where there would be quite a bit of wood coming through. Sometimes the timber came down whole, and it was at those times when we would be especially alert. I thought that at any time I might see a piece of..." Ben looks at Cindy. She has the beginning of a frown on her face. He is not sure if he should continue. "Cindy, I'm sorry. I didn't think this would upset you."

Cindy is not sure what she is feeling. She doesn't know if it is just the fact that she will be twenty-five years old in a few weeks, or if it is the season, or that two days before she had found what seemed to be tiny lines at the corner of each eye. (At which time she laughed at herself and thought, *well now, the bloom is not long for this rose.*) She is not sure just exactly what is going on inside. What she does know is that for some reason Ben's act of placing a straw in her drink made her want to cry.

"No, no, Ben." Cindy speaks with a thick voice, "It's just that I..." She brings her hand up to her mouth. "May I use your restroom?" She doesn't wait for Ben to answer but rushes into the bathroom and closes the door. Inside she buries her face in a towel, still damp, which smells of after-shave lotion. The need to cry passes but she keeps the towel pressed to her face. She scolds herself silently, collects her thoughts, and decides what she will say. She flushes the toilet, washes her hands, and comes back out.

"Ben, I was just thinking. Did they build a memorial for those men?"

Ben is taken aback. "A memorial?"

"Yes, you know, a plaque or something with the date of the cave-in and the names of all those men."

"There is no memorial, Cindy." Ben smiles. "I'm sure I've told that story before and no one has ever asked that question."

Cindy, happy at the thought that not only did she ask a question of Ben but a question that no one else had ever asked before now says, "Why not?"

Ben ponders the question. There were times, he remembers, when the subject of the cave-in was discussed. Usually it was by the older people, the people who had been young when it happened. It was spoken of quietly, a matter not to be lingered upon. Was it respect for the dead? Or was it perhaps some prohibition on the matter imposed by the company? And, now that he thinks about it, he could not recall hearing anyone else except the people of Heaven Hill discuss it at all.

"Well, I can't answer that question. I mean, there is no memorial to those men but as to why not I can't say. It would have been right, of course. Those men came from the other side of the world to die there. The only memorial I recall was a tribute to the founders of the company. It was on a plaque embedded into the concrete at the base of a flagpole…." Ben is silent and turns his face to look out of the window. Cindy looks at Ben's profile, at the set of his jaw and the faraway look in his eyes. She wonders where his thoughts have taken him.

"Well, Ben, I've enjoyed your conversation, but I must go now. I have to pick up Emily."

Ben stands up and walks to the couch and offers his hand to Cindy, to help her up. Touched by this courtesy, she rises slowly, placing her other hand over his as she does so.

"Thank you so much, Cindy." Ben says as he walks her to the door. "You are a good listener. I'll see you tomorrow?"

Cindy smiles. "Yes, of course."

After Cindy leaves, Ben pulls out his notebook and finds his list of names for Christmas. He writes Cindy's name and tries to think of a dollar amount to place there. Different amounts move through his mind. Two hundred? Three, four, five? Too little? Too much? He closes his eyes thinking of the matter. His mind begins to wander to other things and back again to the Chinese coin and then quickly into sleep.

2/

Ben pauses mid-stride on his way to the bathroom. He stands, unmoving, in the middle of his living room. Cindy's words pop up into his head. *"Was it a good trip?"* As usual, when Ben thinks about Orenville there is never a simple answer and he wonders why that is so. He wonders why his thoughts about home should always be with mixed emotions. He thinks about Sal's words. He thinks about Lady Jane and the man who would come visit her and how she sometimes showed up when someone was sick. He wonders if maybe Sal was mistaken.

Ben takes up his notebook again and finds a blank page and makes a list of the names of the men who used to come to his house. He walks over to his almost-completed book and finds the picture he is looking for. In the old photograph there are seven men, including his father. The men are sitting at a table in the shade of the tree in his side yard and behind the men the sun shines on a rock wall. The men are dressed up as though there has been a wedding or a baptism or a birthday party. Each man, he notices, has a bottle of Acme beer in front of him. That is, all except one. That man's name was Tony Mora. Ben studies the photograph and then turns it over. The date, in smudged and faded ink, is August something 1950 something. The other men are Ben's father, his Uncle Ben, and Sal's father. After a few moments, the other names fall into place: Clemente Ortega, Severo Vidales, and Chano Flores. Ben picks up his magnifying glass and assigns the year as 1953. If so, and as Ben computes the time, it would have been approximately three months after that photograph was taken that Sal's father and Ben's uncle were fired and banished from Orenville.

Ben leans back in his recliner and thinks of Mora. It seems to Ben that he came from Colorado to Orenville as a single man and was a boarder at Maria Luisa's house, which was a couple of houses down from Ben's. Mora later married one of Maria Luisa's daughters, Carmen, who Ben remembered as being quite beautiful and who was the lead singer in the choir at church. They hadn't been married very long, maybe a year, when Tony Mora and some other men went deer hunting in the mountains north of the town. Somehow, Mora became separated from his hunting companions and got lost. A search party was organized. They worked the mountains for a full week, but the lost hunter was never found.

Ben looks at the photograph again and wonders. He can't be sure that any of his thoughts mean anything, but he does know that Sal's words have reawakened old feelings, and they are now clear and strong. He recalls his own memory of the watchman and the person with him that night. Who was that person? What did that mean? His thinking is suddenly energized, and the new thoughts excite him. He says out loud, "What if?" Ben reaches for the telephone and dials Sal's number.

"Sal?"

"Yes, Ben?" Sal's breathing is heavy, as though he's been exercising.

"Sal, I think I know who the informant was."

There is a long pause, with only the sound of Sal's breathing. "What?" Sal finally answers.

"The informant, Sal. I think I know who he was." There is another pause, followed by a muffled sound as though Sal has covered the mouthpiece with his hand. "Sorry, Ben, I was kind of tied up here." Ben thinks he hears the sound of a woman's voice. At any other time, Ben would have apologized and ended the conversation, but now his excitement moves him forward.

"It was Tony Mora, Sal."

"Who is...?" Sal begins, but then he says, "Hold on, Ben. I'll be up in a couple of minutes."

Ben stands up and walks to his door, opens it, and steps out on the balcony. He takes several deep breaths. Then he walks back to his chair, sits down, and swivels it around to face the front door.

After a few minutes Sal walks in and smiles at Ben.

"Sorry, man, I was..."

Ben waves away the explanation and hands the photograph to Sal. Sal brings it up close to his face and studies it. The old familiar faces bring a bright smile to his face, it feels as though someone has handed him a piece of his youth.

"Who is the only man not drinking?" Ben speaks those words with a triumphant voice.

Sal, still looking closely at the old photograph, and especially at his own father, says, "Umm ... sorry Ben, is that Tony Mora? God, I hadn't thought of that guy for fifty years." Sal looks at Ben. He notices the agitation. "What is it, Ben?"

"Well, an informant would need to stay sober, you know, to keep an eye out for information to report back to the company."

Sal looks at Ben's face. He's not sure if Ben is serious or not. "What...?"

"Now, those numbers you saw on the list were for someone to investigate, right?"

"Ben, those numbers could have been—"

Ben interrupts. "We can exclude my dad and uncle, your dad, and Chano. So, that leaves Clemente and Severo and Tony Mora. And of those three possibilities only one is not drinking."

Sal laughs. "You're pulling my leg, right? You can't suspect a man because he is not drinking a beer in a fifty-year-old photograph. Maybe he was between beers or maybe he had a hangover or maybe he just didn't like Acme beer. It smelled like hell, from what I can remember. No telling what it tasted like. Old lady Jane was crazy. I don't know what that list and money really meant and neither do you. For all we know she could have placed the money there one day and taken it out the next, or maybe it was meant to help some family out. There were some poor families up there."

Ben continues. Sal's comments have had no effect on him. "Maybe somebody was wise to him. Maybe somebody was ready to blow the whistle on the guy. So, the company tells him, you need to disappear, and it's all arranged. He drifts away from the hunting party and keeps on walking. Somewhere, deep in the woods there is a horse and provisions waiting for him and away he goes. I'll bet you he knew that forest up there like a book. Lost, my eye."

Sal is not sure he is hearing Ben correctly. There is something about his voice and conversation, something new, some kind of agitation just beneath the surface. A vague feeling begins to creep into Sal's chest. He's not sure if it is fear or anger. He proceeds, slowly. "So, Ben, what you're saying is that Tony Mora left one of the most beautiful women in Orenville and a baby boy and just walked away?"

Ben, sitting in his recliner, with his hands crossed over his stomach, says, "That is my conclusion, Sal."

Sal looks at Ben. "That is your *conclusion*?"

Ben leans back on his recliner so that it is fully extended. He closes his eyes and says, "Yes."

Sal has the sudden urge to walk over to Ben, grab him by the collar, and shake him back from wherever he's gone. He subdues the urge and is then filled with regret for having mentioned what he had seen Crazy Jane do. It was merely conversation as far as he was concerned. Something to pass the time on the long drive, a way to entertain Ben back from his dark moods, funny stories to make him laugh.

Sal looks away for a moment and then sits down on the couch. "Listen to me, Ben. Think about what you have just said. It can't be right. You are accusing a dead man of conduct for which you have no proof whatsoever. You are letting your emotions about Dome get the best of you. Suppose, Ben, just for the sake of argument, those numbers Crazy Jane left there were house numbers. How could that make any sense? Of what use could those numbers be? Why would she have to tell anyone in our midst about any house numbers? Hell, that person would know who lived in which house. Those numbers could have just as easily been box numbers or biblical passages, for God's sake. Who knows with a crazy person?" Sal stops, thinking of what he should say next. Ben, sitting perfectly still in his chair, opens his eyes and then closes them again.

"Ben, please. Could there have been an individual or two up there who gave information to the company? I'd rather not think about that but yes, of course. Looking back down all the years an incident here and there could be explained by someone relaying information back to the company. And, I say, so what? In the end, what difference does it make? Think about it, Ben. What kind of company would stoop to that level? What kind of mentality would it take to gather information on hardworking men, the men who did all the dirty and dangerous work that had to be done? You tell me."

Sal stops. He takes a deep breath and goes on. "Come on, man. We knew that company, knew how it worked. The town was exactly the way they wanted it to be. We dealt with it and went on and lived our lives. There are corporations who will clean up with one hand and pollute with the other. I give them credit for at least trying. And, other corporations do good works. But Dome wielded its power as it saw fit and in any direction it wanted to go. They answered to no one. We can say it didn't have to be that way all day long, but that's exactly the way it was."

Ben opens his eyes and slides his recliner back to the seating position. He smiles. "Did you say biblical passages, Sal?"

Sal holds his anger. "Damn it, Ben."

Ben's smile changes, almost to a sneer. "What do you know about it, Sal? You quit and left."

Two clear memories flash through Sal's mind. The first is of the day his father came home and told the family he'd been fired. It was as though the sun had suddenly gone behind a cloud. His grandmother cried and walked out of the living room, but his mother kept her eyes locked on his father's face for a long time as though the words were too difficult to understand and then she buried her face in her hands. Three days later, on the day that Sal's father and Ben's uncle left Orenville, a large group of friends gathered to say their good-byes. At the time, it seemed to Sal that all of Heaven Hill turned out.

The other was of the day he left town to join the Army for the second time. It was the feeling he had on the bus bound for Phoenix to be sworn in. He felt free. It was funny in a strange way because he knew exactly what he was getting in to. The military. The place where regimentation was a way of life. A place where you were told what to do and how to do it for every aspect of your life right down to the exact and precise position of each and every toiletry item in your footlocker. And God help you if on inspection some old sergeant found one of those items in the wrong place. And still, in view of his personal knowledge and experience with the Army way of life, he felt liberated at leaving the town behind him.

Now he laughs dryly. "Yes, you're right, Ben. I quit and left. You know much more about Orenville than I do."

Ben shifts around in his chair. He is suddenly uncomfortable. His mouth feels dry and he is very thirsty. "So, Sal, are we still going out to eat tonight?"

Sal stares at Ben for a long moment. His anger has been replaced with sadness. He looks at his old friend sitting there. The shadow of an even deeper sorrow moves inside of him. Sal manages a smile. "Yes, Ben. Have you called Helen?"

"I am getting ready to call her now."

"Okay, I'll see you then." Sal turns and walks toward the door. He pauses as though he is going to say something else but then walks out and closes the door behind him. Ben waits a few moments and then opens a drawer on his roll top desk and takes out his old Bible. He places it unopened in his lap. It feels heavy. He closes his eyes.

It is a strange blue dusk in the dream and Ben is walking along the narrow road that ran through the concrete ruins of the old mill. He turns to the side and follows a passageway that twists and turns through various tall chambers. Inside of the mill the old walls give off a pale, bone-like glow. He is following a woman in a blue velvet dress. She is always slipping away behind a pillar or a broken wall too far ahead of him to catch up. He follows her into deep areas of the old mill on a winding path he never knew existed. He passes through a long dusty walkway where on either side there are small, shallow rooms built into the old crumbling concrete. Families live in those rooms and some of the people are cooking dinner. Or, they seem to be cooking but when Ben looks closer, he sees that they are holding blackened skillets over old cooking fires that have no flame. Children in rags languish about in the dust. Ben hears a voice in his head. The voice is deep and powerful. *You must tell these people that they are dead.* No one notices him. Then, far ahead, the woman turns to look at him. The color of her skin is the same pale glow of the walls of the mill. There is something familiar about the way she passes her hand across her brow and beckons him. He follows the woman down through a hole in the floor....

A loud noise startles Ben out of his dream and he jumps quickly from the chair. The Bible flies up and lands on the floor. He steps over it and goes into the kitchen. He holds onto the counter as a strange kind of dizziness comes over him, as though he is tumbling along. The musty smell of the old mill is all around him and his legs feel stiff and heavy. He pours himself a full glass of water and drinks it and pours himself another. He looks at his wristwatch, composes himself, and then dials Helen's number from the wall phone in his kitchen. Before the telephone begins to ring, he hangs up. He drinks the second glass of water, takes a few deep breaths, and dials again.

Helen answers on the first ring. They speak for a while and she readily agrees to dinner. She tells him something funny and he laughs. Ben feels better. Just before dialing he was certain she would say no.

22

It is a cold evening. The air is damp, as though there could be snow further north in the mountains behind the city. The couples are having drinks and waiting for a table in the lounge of the Sagebrush Saloon and Grill that is decorated with strings of small Christmas lights. Behind the bar, on shelves of polished mesquite wood, there are the various bottles of different types of whisky, bourbon, gin, and scotch. The top shelf is reserved for a row of bottles of tequila ranging in price from medium to expensive to very expensive.

Sal has been entertaining the ladies by telling them funny stories about his adventures during the time he drove the tour bus down into Mexico. Several times the ladies have burst out in laughter.

Sophie smiles at Sal. "Oh, Sal, can that really have happened?" She takes a sip of her drink. Ben notices for the first time that Sophie speaks with a slight lisp. He also notices that she brings her drink up to her mouth without dipping her head in the slightest. Sal told Ben that Sophie's first husband was very rich and that he'd died at the early age of forty and left her a great deal of money. Sal told Ben that Sophie's next two husbands tried to get their hands on her money, unsuccessfully.

Ben directs his attention to Helen. He's never seen her look so beautiful. She is wearing a green sweater with a black skirt. She is wearing a small cameo brooch and her hair shines in the glow of the Christmas lights. Ben glances at Sophie. She is wearing a red sweater on which there is also a brooch of what look to be diamonds and amethysts.

Sal signals for the waitress to bring another round of drinks. Ben is drinking Mexican beer. The women are having margaritas, and Sal is drinking tequila over ice.

Sal looks at Ben, studying him for a moment. Ben's troubling mood and behavior of the afternoon seem to have passed and Sal is relieved. He clears his throat. "Ben, do you think I should tell the ladies that story about the time I went out to the Hickson place looking for work?"

"Old lady Hickson?" A vision of the old lady comes into Ben's mind. She was a heavy-set spinster who lived alone on a ranch back behind the town of Orenville. "What story would that be, Sal?"

"You know, the time I went out there and she held me hostage." Sal removes a new pack of cigarettes from his coat pocket. He opens it and offers a cigarette to Sophie and Helen and then to Ben. He lights the ladies' cigarettes, lights his, and offers his lighter to Ben. Ben notices that it is gold plated and new and has three small diamonds on each side. Ben isn't sure he remembers that particular story about Miss Hickson or any of the several others told by the kids back then. The stories always seemed to grow from one telling to the next. Ben has no doubt Sal has his own versions. "I'm not sure Sal, but yes, go ahead."

Sal smiles and glances first at Sophie and then at Helen. "A couple of miles behind Orenville there was this old farmhouse. The place had been a working cattle ranch years back but old man Hickson sold all his cattle and most of his land before he died. The people in town said Miss Hickson had been thrown from a horse some years before and hit her head on a rock. She was a large woman." Sal takes a puff of his cigarette. "I have often wondered about that horse."

Sophie chuckles as the waitress arrives with the tray of drinks and announces that it will be a half-hour wait to be seated in the dining room. "Go on, Sal." Sophie smiles at him.

"Okay, so one Saturday morning I went out there because some of the kids at school told me the old lady needed help sometimes and that she paid well. The farmhouse sat a couple of hundred feet from the road. There was a tall wire fence all the way around. I arrived at the gate and I called out, hey, Miss Hickson, do you have any work? Right away, two dogs came running out from behind the house madder than hell, barking and snarling and carrying on. One of the dogs was wearing a black bow tie. I heard a voice coming from the screen porch, 'Who are you?'

"Sal, Sal Madrid, I yelled back."

'Salamander? What kind of name is that?'

"No, I called back, Sal Madrid. You know, like the city in Spain."

In a louder voice she said, 'Salamander Sitting Pain? What is that? Is that some kind of Indian name?' I thought maybe she was hard of hearing and the sound of barking dogs wasn't helping matters any. I yelled out over the sound of the dogs, Miss Hickson, can you call off your dogs? There was a pause and then she called out for Stars and Stripes to come back."

Sophie laughs and says, "Sal, you are making that up, right?"

"Making what up?"

"The names of those dogs."

"Those were the names. Ben here can tell you that her mule, which she used to hitch up to her buggy when she came into town, was named Flag." Sophie glances at Ben. It seems to him that the old lady had a different name for the mule each time she came to town, and Flag may have been one of them. He remembers the canvass covered buggy coming around the curve of the road behind Queen Hill. From the vantage point of Heaven Hill, the white canvass of the wagon looked like a small cloud moving slowly down to the plaza. Miss Hickson was clearly unstable and the people of Orenville gave her plenty of room. She tended to carry on long conversations with herself about this or that can of vegetables or other groceries she was selecting at the company store. Ben smiles and nods at Sophie.

Sal takes a sip of his drink and says, "This is damn good tequila."

"So?" Sophie twirls the diamond ring on her finger, waiting.

"So, what?"

"So, go on with your story."

"Right. So, Miss Hickson invites me up to the porch. 'You, Salamander,' she says, 'what do you want?' I tell her that I am looking for work. She asks me what kind of work and I say anything, you know, cleaning up and stuff. Her voice goes up a notch or two and her eyes turn a bit wild looking. 'Does my house look like it needs cleaning up?' I hadn't seen the inside of her house so I didn't know the answer to that question, but I thought about it and figured you can't say yes to something like that. No ma'am, I say, but right then I am also thinking that maybe it wasn't such a good idea to go out there in the first place. It's obvious the old lady is a little off and kind of strange just like some people said she was. So, I start to back away down the steps of the porch. But just as I start backing down the first step, Miss Hickson says, 'Hold on there, Mr. Salamander.' And down at the bottom of the steps, Stripes, the one with the bow tie, growls, and his growl says to me quite clearly: You ain't going nowhere, Mr. Salamander. That is, unless you don't mind getting there with half an ass."

Sal pauses and looks from Sophie to Helen, who are both laughing. The sound of Helen's laughter pleases Ben.

"Well, I step back up to the porch and Miss Hickson says, 'Salamander, would you care for some lunch?' I'm thinking that it's been a long walk out to that ranch, and I could stand a bite to eat. And besides, I'm not sure what the old lady would say if I refused, so I say yes, and she leads me into her kitchen which is very large. There is a long dining table with long benches on each side. She glances at the table and says a few words that I can't quite make out. 'Have a seat,' she says. I sit down at the nearest end of one of the long benches and immediately she tells me not to sit there because that is John's spot. I move down a space or two and she yells at me that that is William's spot and this goes on from spot to spot until I have moved all the way down one bench and have started back around on the next bench and she has run out of common names and is into names that sound like Jebbity, Bebbity and Lebbity. Well, I get the impression she's just giving me a hard time. I start to backtrack to see if she still has the names right. It looks like she does. Then I try to split the difference and instead of moving a full space, I only move a few inches. 'Ha,' she yells at me, 'do you really think you can squeeze in between Cornwall and Cob?'"

Sophie laughs. "Oh, Sal."

Sal goes on. "Ma'am, I say finally, why don't you just tell me where to sit? 'You know where you are supposed to sit,' she says. No I don't, I say, and she says that I most certainly do. Well, I've had enough of playing musical spaces when I see this little footstool in a corner. It is maybe a foot high. I walk over and sit there. The old lady seems okay with that except she tells me to sit up straight and then asks me if I would like a pork chop sandwich. Sure, I say, why not?"

Laughing, Sophie holds up her hand as though she wants to say something. Sal smiles at her and goes on.

"So, no sooner does Miss Hickson say pork chop sandwich when a pig comes running into the kitchen through a hole in the screen door. He's a fat little guy and he is wearing a red and white polka dot bandanna. His belly almost touches the floor. He walks right up to me. The pig and I are eye to eye. 'Salamander,' the old lady says, 'I would like you to meet Junior.' Your pig's name is Junior? I ask. 'That's right,' she says, 'Junior P. Cuffington the Third.' She lowers her voice and shields her mouth away from the pig. 'But he likes to be called Sheriff. He won't answer if you call him Junior. Just so you know.' I look at Miss Hickson, trying to decide how far I can go with this. I have a bunch of questions, but she gives me a hard look like daring me to dispute the fact that this little pig I am looking at could prefer to be called one thing or another. No telling where it might lead if I get into that with her. So, Junior or Sheriff, whatever."

Sal blows a perfect smoke ring that hangs briefly over his head like a halo. Then he goes on. "But my mind starts to go off on its own, and I'm not sure about what I've gotten in to. I start to get a strange feeling about the old lady and the whole situation, and I really, really don't think it's a good idea to eat a pork chop sandwich in front of a pig. Nope, not at all. I mean, are that pork chop and little Junior related? I'm thinking they probably are and if that's the case then it would be very disrespectful of me to accept that sandwich. Heck, it could be his daddy or second cousin or something. I look at Junior's homely face. I don't want to offend him. Miss Hickson, I say, I appreciate your offer, but I don't think I could eat that sandwich in front of Junior, here.

"Miss Hickson looks at me and says, 'You'll eat it and like it.' And the pig, acting as though he knows what's going on, becomes agitated and starts to run around in circles kicking up his hind legs to beat the band.

"Miss Hickson puckers up her lips and coos, 'That's my pretty little buckaroo Sheriff, yes he is.' Then she says it again.

"Well, this bit of attention only serves to further excite Junior, whose hooves are tapping out quite a rhythm on that linoleum floor. And now I notice he has a toy badge pinned to his bandanna. I want to laugh but I don't dare. I'm thinking I have to find a way out of that place. I feel trapped and I start to get desperate. I say, Miss Hickson, I am sorry, but the last time I had a pork chop sandwich I broke out in this real bad rash. She waved one big arm at me that said she didn't care one bit about that. I went on quickly. Please, ma'am, I had to be hospitalized and I missed a lot of school. That part was okay with me but then they said if that rash reached my heart I could die, so they had to give me a bunch of shots in a circle around my stomach to keep that from happening. The old lady still said nothing, but it made Junior stop his dancing and look at me and snort twice, kind of like a laugh. Then he started up again. Please, Miss Hickson, I'm serious. I almost died. The shots didn't work, and it got so bad that the doctors had to call my family to come to the hospital to say their last goodbyes. They all came into my room dressed in black, even my best friend Ben, except that his black pants were sort of high waters as we say up on Heaven Hill and I could see he was wearing white socks and that upset me a lot since I had told him many times not to do that. That is, not to wear white socks with black pants and I was trying to object to such a sight but my poor old grandmother came over and put her hand over my mouth, a little too tightly I might add, and told me not to speak and save my strength for my last Act of Contrition and the doctor had to tell Ben to leave, seeing as how he was upsetting me so. Get out, he said."

Ben laughs. Sal smiles and laughs also and goes on. "'Stop,' the old lady said, 'I have never heard such nonsense. The way you carry on.' Then she kind of squinted at me and said that I reminded her of someone, but she couldn't figure out who it was. I kept on talking. Please, Miss Hickson, if I have to eat that sandwich could you at least ask Junior to step outside? Well, the look I get from the old lady is like I have suggested that she take Junior out to the back yard and shoot him. It is entirely out of the question. Furthermore, her stare seems to say, I had just better watch my mouth in making any more statements along those lines. Step outside indeed. Her little buckaroo sheriff is staying put. It's his world around here and I'd better learn to deal with it.

"The old lady removes a plate from the refrigerator and turns on the stove. Little Junior stops his cavorting and looks at me and then back at the stove. I'm thinking that when I do get that sandwich, I can just take one bite and then act like I'm choking and maybe Miss Hickson will tell me that if I can't eat a pork chop sandwich like a regular human being then I could just get on back home and take my sissy throat and scrawny little butt with me.

"Ma'am, I say, I had a big stack of pancakes for breakfast and I'm not hungry at all. She ignores me. Miss Hickson, I say, I notice that Junior is wearing a bandanna. She starts to turn around. It's a slow process. 'So?' she says. So, I say, maybe you could pull it up over his eyes. 'Can't do that,' she says, 'but I can put a blindfold on you.' She pulls out a handkerchief from her apron pocket and takes a step in my direction. Please Miss Hickson, I say, I don't know what good that would do. I mean, he, Junior, will still see me. And that's the important part, not that I can't see him but that he can't see me eating that pork chop sandwich, you know, just in case there's some kind of family connection going on here.

"Miss Hickson screams at me. 'Blindfold Junior? In his own house? How dare you?' And then she reaches into the skillet and pulls out her so-called pork chop and flings it at me. Well, it's not a pork chop after all. It's a weenie flying across that wide kitchen, and when I see that it's only a weenie, I think I can eat probably that, and Junior shouldn't mind. I reach out to grab it when the pig jumps up and snatches it out of mid-air and swallows it in one bite. Gulp, he says, and licks his lips."

Sal takes a drink, savors it for a moment, and looks away as though he is done with the conversation. Then he comes back. "So, the impression I am getting about our little sheriff here is that he couldn't care less what you eat in front of him as long as he gets his cut. It doesn't matter if it's a pork chop sandwich, a baloney sandwich, or a bacon burro flying through the air. It's all the same to him. Bring it on, he says. That's what I'm thinking. What I am also thinking is that if Miss Hickson is going to be tossing any more weenies, I had better be on my toes. So, I stand up. I'm thinking I'll have the height advantage on Junior when the next weenie flies. Sure enough, I can see there is another weenie in the skillet. 'Who said you could leave the table?' Miss Hickson says. 'Sit down.'

"Ma'am, I say, as patiently as I can, I am not sitting at any table. You told me that all the places were taken. 'That's right,' she says, 'they are.' Well? I say. 'Well, what?' she says. Well, how can I be leaving a table if I wasn't sitting there in the first place? 'Ohhhh,' she says, 'you *are* a smart one, aren't you? Someone ought to teach you a lesson.' Then she starts to roll up her sleeves. The whole deal is going from bad to worse. So, to kind of change the subject, I say, hey, Miss Hickson, your little Junior sure is smart, isn't he? I mean, you know, catching a weenie in the air and all that. I have never seen a pig do that. I smile up at her. Did you teach him that trick?"

The waitress brings another round of drinks and laughs along with the ladies and Ben. Sal goes on. "Well, big old Miss Hickson does not look like she is at all happy about my compliment. In fact, it looks like my praise is having the opposite effect. She seems to be angry that I could suggest such a thing. So, now she is rolling up her sleeves in earnest and all the while looking around for something handy to smack me with. She turns off the stove in an obvious gesture that says very clearly that her hospitality is over. In the meantime, I am looking at the hole in the screen door to see if maybe I can scoot out that way. Then I start to think that if she does smack me, I might go flying out the door and get a running start on Stars and Stripes. So, a smack from her might not be all bad.

"So, the old lady finishes with her sleeves and says to me, 'Do you know what you do?' No ma'am, I answer. 'You,' she says, 'remind me of Cautious Bob.' Who? I ask. 'Cautious Bob,' she repeats. 'And don't act like you don't know him.' Her voice starts to go up.

"I have no idea who Cautious Bob is, so I say so. That upsets her a great deal. She insists that I most certainly do know who Cautious Bob is. She says I am lying. No ma'am, I say, I know Ben, he of the atrocious white socks, and Danny and Ray. And I also know Chalo, Chapo, and Chico who always hang around together, and then there's that new guy they call *Chiplón* who doesn't hang around with anybody and who, now that I think about it, looks quite a bit like Junior over there. And then of course there's Lalo and Lito who are sort of friends, and Licho and Lencho, who can't stand each other. I know all of those guys for sure, and sometimes I wish I didn't, but there you go, and….

"'SHUT YOUR TRAP WITH ALL THAT NONSENSE!' She screamed. 'You make me so mad I could spit.' She walks over to me. 'Cautious Bob,' she tells me through clenched teeth, 'is that mangy no-good chicken-thief bobcat who is always sneaking around here trying to grab my Peep LaRue, and he thinks he is real smart too. You act just like him. Are you denying that you know him?' Yes, I am, I say. And by the way, Miss Hickson, who or what is your Peep LaRue? The old lady yells at me that Peep LaRue is her prize cock, as if I didn't know.

"Hold on there, I'm thinking. Come on, now. This is not going in any direction I'd like to go. No way. I had started out with high expectations on that fine Saturday morning. I had hopes of earning some money but things started to go downhill at the gate and now a pig had beaten me to a flying weenie and on top of all that I was being compared to some mangy chicken-stealing bobcat and accused of lying about it.

"So, I was insulted and indignant about the whole thing, but I was also wondering about that prize cock. I mean, what did a prize rooster look like anyway? A lot of people up on Heaven Hill had chickens and roosters but they all looked the same to me. I was interested to know what a prize rooster would look like. Was he a prize rooster because he had a great big old beak or a real long neck or what? Maybe you could see that guy's neck from a long way off, a mile maybe. I had visions about that. I'd heard rumors that there were cockfights in some corrals back in the hills behind the ranch. It could be that he was a prize fighting cock, like a champion or something.

"Miss Hickson, I say, maybe I could meet Peep LaRue. Well, all I get for my interest in her prize cock is a very hard glare. 'Ha,' she says, 'I'll just bet you would.' She goes on, 'Yes, I'll bet you would like that, wouldn't you?' Yes ma'am, I say, I would like it. I was being honest about it. I was interested in that prize rooster. She had said that I would like it and I was agreeing with her. I was being polite. But there was some kind of miscommunication going on. Miss Hickson's eyes were getting small and beady. I thought she might slap me any second, and I didn't know why. She said it again, slowly, with a pause between each word about how much I would like to see her Peep LaRue. Well, I finally get the picture that what she is saying is sort of the opposite of what she means. So, I say no, I do not want to meet Peep LaRue after all. I have changed my mind. Well, this really aggravates her, and she yells at me that Peep LaRue doesn't want to meet me either and as a matter of fact, just so I know exactly where I stand in the matter, Mr. LaRue wouldn't be caught dead meeting the likes of me. Her voice gets low and crackly. 'I should've known. Coming around here with your fancy name. Acting like you're too good to eat my pork chop sandwich when all along all you really wanted was to grab my Peep. Isn't that right? Ha! Ha! How about Peepeegrabber? That would be more like it. Yeah. Mister Salamander Peepeegrabber the Fifth, Sixth, and Seventh.'

"Hold it right there Miss Hickson, I say. Let's get one thing straight. I came out here looking for honest work, period. Now, if the best you can do with my name is Salamander, I guess I can live with that. But I'm telling you right now I did not come out here to grab anybody's, you know, whatever. Prize or not. Now my friend Ben, he...maybe, but never mind about that. So, if it's all the same to you, I'll just be on my way."

Sal takes a sip of his drink and goes on. "The old lady starts out with a scream but then her voice mellows down to normal conversation. 'Do you think you can just come over here and leave whenever you please?' Yes, I say, it's a free country. 'Well you are dead wrong, mister. We've got rules about that. You wait right here while I get my rulebook. Keep your eyes on him Sheriff, don't let him get away.'

"Well, after she left the room, I started to walk toward the door, but Junior blocked my way. I tried to fake him this way and that, but he was up to the task. I laughed. I had never met a watch pig before. I went back and sat down and then Junior came over and started to snuggle up to me. His breath smelled like weenie. I wasn't mad or anything about him beating me to that weenie. Heck, any pig that can jump that high deserves to win. I don't want to be a sore loser. So, I petted him for a bit and then, just for the heck of it, I slipped his bandana up over his snout. He shook his head about it, but I figured he was just being coy. I tied it securely so it wouldn't fall off. I had created a little pig bandit. A pig bandit with a badge. Miss Hickson was gone for a while so Junior and I had a chance to play around. I chased him around the kitchen for a few laps.

"I have no idea what happened but all of a sudden Junior just keeled over. He was running along pretty good a few steps ahead of me when he fell. He slid along the linoleum floor and crashed into the wall. Oh, man, I think, I've killed Junior. I go over to him to remove the bandana from his snout and notice that his ears are twitching, and his eyes are crossed. In a second or two he came around and his eyes focused on me. He jumped up and peed on the floor. He backed away from me squealing and peeing and keeping his eyes on me all the way out the door."

The cocktail waitress comes by and informs the couples that their table is ready.

Sal goes on. "Miss Hickson never came back. Maybe she forgot all about me. I went over to the stove and got the other weenie and walked out of the kitchen door. Stars and Stripes were looking at Junior, way up on a hill, still running. I threw the weenie at their feet and hit the road.

"I was disappointed I never got to see Peep LaRue. No telling what he looked like. But as far as Cautious Bob was concerned, I didn't think he was real. That poor old lady was just plain off. There was still a problem though, but closer to home. I had seen a weenie disappear in mid-air, just like that. So, I was thinking that someone should warn Mr. Peeps about the situation. Sooner or later he could be strutting around that yard catching some rays and minding his own business when that so-called sheriff might take that long prize neck as some kind of gift-wrapped weenie and give it a shot."

Sal looks over at Sophie. She stops laughing and speaks. "Oh Sal, could there really have been people that…quaint in Orenville?"

Sal laughs. "Yes, ma'am. If that's what you want to call them. Whole families of them, and they all lived along the curve of the road above Ben's house. Very quaint, actually. But you'd better move along quickly when you heard that first shout and try your best not to get caught in the middle when they started up with their quaintness." Ben laughs. Sophie and Helen laugh also as they walk away to the restroom.

"How do you feel, Ben?"

"I feel good." Ben laughs again at Sal's story. "I'm glad I came."

Sal smiles. "You should try this tequila, Ben. It's smooth as silk." Sal swirls his drink. In the soft light the liquid in his glass has a golden glow.

"Yeah, Sal, maybe I will. Like someone said, here in this place and time, right?

"Glad to hear you're getting the picture, old buddy."

23

The couples are seated at a table by a window that looks out to the rain-washed patio where golden leaves lay scattered about on the rustic tile floor. White chairs lean on white tables, and on the edges of the patio there are a few Christmas lights on the branches of the trees. It has been a pleasant meal, full of laughter and conversation about childhood experiences. Now, Ben begins to hear the sound of music coming from the lounge. The song they are playing is one that is not familiar to him. Listening closely, he finally finds the string of the song and begins to follow it. The music is unpredictable in its melody. It seems to be an altogether new and different kind of tune that still manages to hint somehow at memories of other songs in Ben's mind. A woman's voice, unlike any other Ben has ever heard, begins to sing a song in French. Excusing himself, Ben stands up from the table and walks behind the partition to the lounge. He stands off to one side and then the singer turns toward him, and her eyes meet his. For a few moments she sings to him.

Ben returns to the table and smiles at Helen. "I'm sorry, I've never heard a voice like that." Helen smiles and places her hand over his.

Sal laughs. "What did I tell you, Ben? A voice like liquid silver, right?" Sal turns to Sophie. "Sophie, my dear, you speak French. What is she saying?"

Sophie laughs. "It is much too sad to repeat."

"Please," Ben says.

Sophie listens. "Well, she sings about a man who waits by the window of his room for an old lover to come by to say goodbye for the last time. The autumn leaves swirl on the sidewalk. The woman is leaving, moving to another city far away. He may never see her again. He is remembering when their love was young."

The waiter comes by and places a tray on the table. Along with the check there are four tiny tamales on the tray. Ben discovers that they are confections wrapped in small pieces of cornhusk. They contain a rich dark chocolate enclosed in soft white fudge and they are delicious.

There is something in the singer's voice and song that remind Ben of the humming of his mother as she baked and also of a song China sang to him one early summer night so many years ago. Ben smiles once again at Helen and then at Sophie and begins to speak. "When I was a boy, maybe ten or eleven, I began to have toothaches. My mother would place an aspirin on the tooth and that would relieve the pain somewhat. After a while the toothaches got so bad that my dad had to take me to the dentist. As it turned out there were actually two molars that were badly decayed. The dentist said that he would have to pull them out but at the hospital where they would need to put me to sleep. He told my father to drive me up to the hospital where he would meet us. I was afraid. The thought of being put to sleep terrified me.

"We arrived at the hospital and a nurse took me into a room with a bed. Another nurse came in and then the dentist. The second nurse placed a mask over my mouth and told me to close my eyes and breathe deeply. I was not completely out but neither could I open my eyes. It seemed to me that the dentist placed a device into my mouth and began to turn a handle on it. The purpose of that device was to open my mouth as wide as possible and at the point where I thought they could not force my mouth open any wider without breaking my jaw, they opened it further still. Then the blackness swept over me."

Ben pauses, he had never been sure if his memory of the

incident was correct or not, but he had felt as though he was going to die if he didn't wake up, so he had forced himself to wake up.

"Yes, Ben, go on." Ben releases the memory and looks into Helen's eyes.

"Yes, well, afterward, when my father drove me home, my jaw hurt so much that I couldn't open my mouth." Ben listens to the last notes of the song, then continues. "My uncle had been home that weekend and he'd asked my mother to make tamales for him. Sometimes in the making of tamales there would be some of the filling and batter left over. That is, the person making them would run out of the cornhusks in which they were wrapped. What they would do then is make *pan perdido*, which means lost bread. In English it is called tamale pie.

"It was snowing when my father drove me home from the hospital that evening. When we walked into the kitchen, there was the *pan perdido* fresh out of the oven. I was hungry and the aroma of it made me even more so, but I couldn't open my mouth to eat any. I was able to communicate to my mother to save some for me, but I still couldn't open my mouth enough to chew anything on the next day or the day after that. By then the tamale pie was all gone and the occasion for the making of it never arose again.

"Years later I told my wife that story and right away she made some for me. I really thought it would satisfy the old hunger and it was good but not the same for some reason. I don't know why. Maybe it is that nothing can compare to your memory." Ben looks out of the window to the patio. "There are times even now when I can see it. I can see that golden pie in the center of the table in that bright kitchen on that evening so clearly I can smell it." Ben laughs. "It's funny what we choose to remember, isn't it?" He rubs his eyes for a few moments as the notes of another song begin in the lounge. Then he looks at Helen. "Would you like to dance, Helen?"

Helen squeezes his hand. "I would love to, Ben."

24

B en's book is finished. It is now in the hands of the publishing company where they are to print five hardbound copies. He has decided that he will keep one of the books, give one to Sara, another to Sal, and one he intends to donate to the Orenville Public Library. He's not sure to whom he'll give the last copy.

Ben's efforts on his pictorial history occupied much of his time and energy over the past three years and now that it is finished, he feels a vague emptiness. It's as though a part of him has walked out the door. And, to add to the emptiness, both Sal and Helen are gone. Sal has gone to Louisiana to meet Sophie's family, and Helen has gone to Minnesota to visit her daughter and granddaughters who were not able to come to Arizona for Christmas after all.

The weather has been overcast and cold and gloomy for the past week and Ben hasn't ventured out except for a late lunch. Now, he walks from room to room in his apartment, not exactly sure why he is doing so or what it is he is looking for. He thinks that maybe he was looking for stationary to write a letter to Sara. Ben finds the paper and a pen and returns to the kitchen table. He pours himself a cup of hot coffee into which he pours a shot of brandy. He thinks for a few moments and begins to write.

Dear Sara,

Ben looks at the salutation. It looks strange to him. *Should it be Dear Sara or Sara Dear?* Ben puts the pen down and drinks his coffee. He raises his hand to his chin and is surprised to find he forgot to shave that morning. He goes into the bathroom where he fumbles briefly with his electric shaver before he can plug it into the outlet. As he shaves and studies his face in the mirror, a slight pounding comes and goes in his ears and his balance feels a little off. He thinks about Sal's numbers. They are suddenly very interesting to him. He speaks to the reflection in the mirror. "Chapter and verse?"

Ben picks up his Bible from the lower shelf of an end table by the couch and walks back into the kitchen. Inside the cover is a folded sheet of paper where he had written the numbers from Sal's story about Lady Jane. Ben looks at the numbers: 217, 218, and 319. He opens his Bible to Genesis and reads Chapter 2, verse 17. He ponders the words. Then he reads verse 18, and then Chapter 3, verse 19. Ben adds more brandy to his coffee and reads about the tree of knowledge, and that man should not live alone, and that Adam ate of the tree, and because of that it would be from the sweat of his brow that he would eat his bread until he returned to dust. Ben reads on, using different combinations of the numbers.

Ben looks out of the arcadia door. He is surprised to see that it is dark. He looks at the sheet of paper again where he had previously made three notations. The first was "house numbers" which he had scratched out, then there was a notation "biblical passages" which he now marks out. The third entry reads "employee numbers."

Ben determines that the numbers 217 and 218 would signify that two individuals were hired on the same day. "Sal and I were hired on the same day." Ben repeats those words several times. He looks closely at the two numbers. He speaks again. "Two plus one plus seven equals ten." Then he adds the digits in the second number. "Two plus one plus eight equals eleven." Then, the third number. "Three plus one plus nine equals thirteen." The numbers spin around in his head. "Ten, eleven, thirteen. Why is twelve missing?" For a moment, the fact that the number twelve is missing is of great concern to him. It's as though something important has been taken away.

Ben stares at a blank wall for a long time, then he starts to pace from room to room. A vague feeling begins to rise in him. Something is rolling and tumbling around his head, as though a great mystery is about to be revealed. Then it comes, he has found the number twelve.

Ben is certain the number twelve signifies the twelve apostles. He stumbles back into the kitchen and begins to read the New Testament. The words jump around on the page. The room begins to spin. Ben lays his head down on his arms on the table and falls asleep.

25

When Ben wakes up in the morning, he is surprised to find that he fell asleep at the kitchen table. The quart of brandy is empty. As the memory of the previous day and night begins to move around in the corners of his mind, he feels ashamed. He'd meant to use his time alone wisely. His plan was to maintain his regimen and read a new book and write to Sara. Instead, he'd wasted his time on an act of foolishness that now makes him cringe. He vows to not pursue the matter any further and to remind himself of that vow he slides a rubber band over his wrist. Ben runs a hot bath and gets into the tub. The hot water is soothing to him and soon he is deep in reverie.

A memory comes by of an early summer day when three families gathered at the river for a picnic bringing with it the sparkling stream flowing in the sunlight and the warm sand on his bare feet and big pieces of ice over beer and pop in large tubs and food cooking over open fires. There was a softball game with cheering and laughter and a watermelon floating in a circle of rocks in the cool water at the edge of the stream.

Then, driving back home later, Ben was thinking about some cliff dwellings the men said were further up the river and how maybe when he got older, he would go and try to find them. When they got back home, Ben realized he'd forgotten his shoes at the river. His father had to take him back down the long dirt road to look for them. Ben spotted them right away and got out of the car to get them. When he got back into the car his father seemed lost and confused, as though he couldn't understand why they were there. It was brief but noticeable.

Ben steps out of the bathtub and puts on his bathrobe. He looks at the open Bible on the kitchen table and the scattered pieces of paper on the table and on the floor. He collects all the sheets of paper and takes them out to the balcony to burn them in the grill. It is cold. Ben feels a chill through his bathrobe on his wet skin. He looks at the flames and remembers other fires in other times. He closes the lid on the grill and walks back inside.

At his desk Ben begins another letter to Sara. His mind is clear. He writes quickly.

Dear Sara,

The last time I saw your grandpa he did not recognize me. He knew he had a son, but in his mind that son was not me. He was very pleasant, and we spoke of many things. He was describing for me the complexity of the original underground mine. When your grandpa first started working at the mine, he was sixteen years old. He was a student in high school, and he would go directly from school to the mine. He worked with Nino Gomez. I don't know if you remember him. He lived along the road by the old mill. Back in the olden days the company would go down to Mexico and recruit men to come up on the train to work in the mine. They also brought Chinese workers from San Francisco. One of Nino's sons, Sammy, was captured by the Germans during the Second World War and held prisoner for some time. The last time I saw Nino he was still alert and sharp. He was into his nineties. I think he is gone by now.

Your grandpa was Nino's helper back then. This would have been in 1925 or 1926. Their job was to move men and supplies from the outside of the mine down to the various tunnels. Each trip down in the

167

cage had to count since space was at a premium. The idea was to take down as much as you brought back up so that there were no wasted trips. The miners were packed into the cage like sardines and the cage dropped fast. The main shaft was almost eight hundred feet deep and the tunnels, at fifty-foot increments of depth, branched out from the main shaft for a very long way. Your grandpa said he thought Nino could operate that hoist with his eyes closed. It would drop down fast and stop on a dime at the exact level of the tunnel to which that particular crew was headed. The crews worked ten-hour shifts and were paid three dollars a day. When I started working for the company, the pay was fifteen dollars a day.

The interesting thing about mining is that you must remove and process much rock to get to the ore. In open pit mining it takes a lot of rock to make a little bit of copper. Some people will not bend down to pick up a penny. They say it is not worth the trouble. I do. I do pick up that penny. That penny could be part of the end product of our front yard on Heaven Hill.

If you cut down a tree, you can plant another. You can take the seed from any harvested crop and plant it and the following year it will yield again. Mining is different. Once you remove a mountain, you can't replace it. Sometimes I wondered back then if in the back of each miner's mind he knew that by removing a part of the earth he was working himself out of a job. No one ever talked about that, but I still wonder.

The Bible says that man will eat by the sweat of his brow, which brings to my mind a particular image. We were laying track on a hot day, a hundred and ten degrees down in the hole. As my partner and I drove the spikes into the railroad ties, the jarring motion of our hammers hitting the spikes would cause the sweat on our foreheads to fly. The drops of sweat would sizzle as they hit the hot rails and quickly evaporate. Neither of us spoke. We had a long way to go.

Speaking of that, it seemed to me that the circumstances were always such that we would work in the depths of the pit where it was the hottest in the summer and up high where the cold wind blew in the winter. We were transported between job sites in what can only be described as cattle trucks. One time in the winter one of the men in our crew rode along with his legs hanging over the side of the crowded truck. Riding that way apparently cut off the circulation to his legs and it was so cold he almost got frostbite. It was seventeen degrees that day and very windy. His name was Jess, his last name will come to me later. I have not thought of him for a long time but now he is very clear. He could throw three pennies up in the air in a row and catch them, one by one with his palm facing out, quick as a cat. He was very funny and had a way of telling a joke that made you start laughing before he got to the punch line. He could make you laugh even if it was a joke you'd heard before. He would give you a look like daring you not to laugh. One time we were riding along in the truck and he turned away from me for a moment. When he turned back to me, he had a thin strip of green cloth sticking out of one of his nostrils. It came down over his moustache to the corner of his mouth. He had a very serious look on his face and told me that he was a dangerous man, just in case I didn't know. He said he was sick and tired of people always looking at him in a certain way and that I could save myself a lot of trouble by staring at someone else's face for a change. He went on to say that any sorry so-and-so who was foolish enough to mess with him on that day had better think the matter all the way through slowly, carefully, and seriously. He said this in Spanish which made it funnier than can be translated. He lived on Crown Hill, which was the hill directly across…

Ben stops writing. He looks up at the picture on the wall. The houses and faces of the families who lived in them begin to pass by. *Walking along the dirt road above his house in the mornings of early summer. The air filled with the smell of the wet ground sprinkled down with water hoses from the houses along the way...then roses, peach blossoms, breakfast...*

Ben shakes himself back to the present and continues writing.

The men there, the miners of Orenville and Stanton, and their wives, gave their all to the mine and their towns. They held nothing back. Those towns were of them and by them and in them. They, those of that generation, are mostly gone now. May they all rest in peace.

Long before it happened the rumors began that in time the ever-expanding open pit would one day devour Heaven Hill and then the rest of Orenville. What I did not realize at the time was that I myself would have a hand in the destruction of Heaven Hill.

One day a man from the company came to your grandpa's house and made his proposal. Your grandpa's house was appraised at five hundred dollars, to be paid when he tore it down and removed it. Each family on Heaven Hill went through the same process and in time all the houses on the mountain were gone. Some of the houses up there had been handed down from father to son for two or three generations.

Ben walked up the main winding road of Heaven Hill. No one lived there anymore. Smoke rose from fires here and there where someone had burned old unsalvageable lumber from the torn-down houses. Ben recited the names of all the families as he walked by the empty places where they used to live.

The first drill with its twenty-foot tall rack appeared around a curve, moving slowly on its tracks as it began the climb up Heaven Hill.

I worked for the drilling and blasting department at that time. When the houses were gone, we began to drill the holes for creating the levels in the expansion of the pit. I saw the first hole being drilled near the top of the hill. The spinning three-headed twenty-inch bit paused briefly above the ground and then entered. Even the hardest rock could not resist.

One day we got to the area around your grandpa's house and began drilling there. Each drill hole was sixty-five feet deep. The holes were loaded with forty-pound bags of explosive. We would load each hole with between thirty to thirty-five bags. When we blasted that section of Heaven Hill, where your grandma's house sat, it exposed a cavity at the bottom of the level wall. It was maybe four feet high by three feet wide by three feet deep. Sometimes when we blasted, it would expose the old tunnels. Those old tunnels interested me, and I was always on the lookout for them.

The rock was very dark in that hollow place and I walked over to get a closer look. Inside the cavity, sticking out from the walls, were clusters of amethyst crystals. Loosened by the blast, they came out easily from the surrounding rock. The smooth, perfect amethyst crystals were dazzling in the sun. I knew that they, along with everything else, would be loaded onto a train and hauled down to the crusher to be pulverized. I put some of the crystal clusters in my lunch pail and took them home and gave them to your mother. Amethyst was her birthstone. She placed them on the sill of the kitchen window of our house on Queen Hill.

I remember Heaven Hill as it was. I remember evenings in the spring and the sound of children playing, evenings made soft by the fragrance of flowers, the laughter of young girls. I remember the games of kick the can; a mother calling her son for supper; the sounds of the radios tuned here and there to Mexican or American stations coming from the open doors and windows, or someone practicing on a saxophone or clarinet or trumpet. As you walked along you could hear Stardust, Cielito Lindo, Trumpeter's Lullaby, Noche de Ronda, A Blossom Fell. I remember summer nights when I would lay on a cot under the stars in our front yard and listen to the sound of the music

coming from the Minero Dancehall. All of these things
I remember very clearly.

Ben pauses. He wonders if he should mention Helen. He
decides to wait until Sara arrives so that he can introduce her in
person. He begins to write again and then pauses again. He thinks
about his circumstances. He thinks about all the things he has and
all the things that have been lost, things that can never again be
replaced or recovered. Ben continues.

> I have often thought about those amethyst crystals.
> For one thing, I wondered about the fact that no one
> before me had ever seen them. They were a hidden
> treasure encased in the darkness of solid rock. I imagine
> now that as I slept in your grandma's house, in the earth
> somewhere below my bed there was the glow of the
> amethyst cave. I imagine this in spite of the fact that
> there would have to be some light for the crystals to glow.
> Although, on the other hand, there was a pocketknife I
> wanted very much that would glow in the dark. It had a
> yellow-green glow. It was for sale in the company store
> up on the third floor in the sporting goods section.

Ben looks at what he has written. He's not sure that's what he
wanted to say. The paragraph is at the top of a fresh page. Ben sets
that page aside and starts another.

> The Minero Dancehall was the social center
> of Heaven Hill and it was one of the first of the old
> buildings up there to be torn down. Back when I was
> a boy it was also a theater where they showed Mexican
> movies. It was also a basketball court. There were
> traveling Mexican troupes who used to perform acts
> there. Those shows were called *comedias*.

Ben begins to draw away as he thinks of the actors and
actresses who made their living going from town to town giving

shows. He remembers the brightly dressed actress who spoke to the boys outside the hall. She was very pretty and spoke with a voice that seemed to carry with no effort. He smiles at the memory and goes on.

Directly above the Minero was a barbershop. There were three barber chairs in it, and it was a busy place, especially on Fridays and Saturdays. I worked as a shoeshine boy there for a while. Some of the jokes they told there were very funny. I would pretend not to hear them since they were not meant for kids but there were times I couldn't help laughing. What was funny was that whenever I would laugh quietly at one of the jokes there would not be much laughter by the men about it. It apparently was not that funny to them. Then there were other jokes for which all the men would erupt instantaneously into raucous laughter that I could not get at all.

One day a man walked in and said he wanted a shoeshine. I forget his name now. He sat in the high chair and I started working on his shoes. We used a wash of leather soap to clean up the shoes before applying the wax on them to shine them up. Well, when I began to apply the wash, I noticed that he had either tried to dye his shoes with some color other than the original color or he had used a black polish on what were originally brown shoes. The longer I worked on those shoes the worse they looked. If I tried black shoe polish the brown would show through, and if I tried brown shoe polish the black would show through. It was a mess. Finally, I tried the neutral shoe polish and I brought the shoes to a high shine. As it turned out either the man didn't notice, or he didn't mind because he paid me and tipped me and walked out of that barbershop with very shiny black and brown polka dot shoes. He was happy with his shoeshine. There were some colorful characters up there. Maybe someday I can tell you something about them.

I remember the football games in the fall. I remember the brightness of the stadium lights, the smell of the grass and the sound of the band.

Ben pauses.

The stadium was down below the old mill. Some people watched the games from up there. They would take their chairs and blankets and watch it from up there.

Ben hurries on.

My book is finally finished and is now at the printer's. It's a relief. When I first started it, I thought it would be simply a matter of pasting pictures on pages but as it grew it became more complicated, especially the notations each picture required. In some of the earliest pictures I have not been able to identify the men in them. This is also true of some of the landscape. Orenville looked different back then. Some of the notations on the back of the old pictures are very faint but I have been able to decipher them using a magnifying glass. Anyway, the job is finally finished, and I am excited and looking forward to seeing the finished product. The book is dedicated to the miners of Orenville and Stanton.

Ben stops writing again and thinks how he will say what he feels needs to be said. He thinks about Cindy's question about memorials and the fact that the only memorial in Orenville was the one honoring the owners. Ben stands up and walks to the sliding glass door and looks out to a patch of blue sky in a break in the clouds. After a few moments the fast-moving clouds cover it up again. Ben returns to his desk and continues his letter.

In the beginning I meant to only write captions for the pictures, but as I became deeper and deeper involved, the captions grew until they became almost like short stories about the subjects. As the project grew, so did my desire to add to the notations because it seemed to me that something else needed to be said. Still, I don't know if what I said was adequate to the task.

Ben pauses again. His thoughts begin to wander and slip away and for a moment his mind goes blank. He stands up again slowly and steps to his front window to look beyond the grounds at the tops of the trees out in the orchard. The branches move in the wind. The world seems cold and gray in the dying light of the late afternoon. A deep tiredness begins to sweep over him. He returns to his desk and sits down.

A memory comes of a teacher in high school. He was very young looking and he was speaking about the town. He made it sound like a different place, somehow. The image passes by. Ben moves on.

Orenville was a town unto itself. It was a place hidden away deep in the mountains where some of the things Americans take for granted had, for some, never quite reached.

Ben pauses. Something seems to be slipping away again, then it returns.

The social lines in Orenville were distinct and deeply drawn. Some say the town was simple and idyllic. Others say it was hard and confining. I guess in the end it was whatever those who lived there say it was, different views from different sides of the lines.

Still, the town and company were bound tightly together and while the place might be held high by some and not so high by others, in the end for all who lived there it was home, and home is where the heart is.

Ben stops and looks at what he has written. He looks up and sits motionless for several minutes. His mind feels completely empty. From somewhere far away the words come in a hoarse whisper. "It was…what it was."

The words bring Ben back. The page looks fuzzy and distant. He bends down close to the paper.

> It's getting late now so I will close. Hugs and kisses for Marie and Margaret.
>
> Love,
> Dad

Ben seals the letter and places a stamp on it. He leans back in his chair and feels the energy leaving his body. He stands with effort and walks out of his apartment into the cold dampness of the evening and attaches the letter to his mailbox. A shiver runs through him as he walks back inside and he raises the thermostat. Slowly, he makes his way to his bedroom.

He undresses and pulls the covers up to his neck and thinks about the heat in late summer in Orenville *and how the humidity would start to rise along with the huge thunderheads to the north and then the lightning and the deafening thunderclaps and the pounding rain on the tin roofs and the power of the rushing water coming down the alley by his house…*

Ben is surprised at the clarity of his thoughts as they pick up speed and race along.

…and the snows of winter and how they would take the pure white snow from the railing of the front porch into a cup and make ice cream with canned milk and sugar and the dark evenings of Lent and yeast bread and salmon croquettes and soupy beans and the howl of the wind on those black nights. The wonderful smell of the bakery by his house. The whine of the saws cutting lumber in the back lot of the lumberyard across the alley and the smell of the freshly cut wood. The trees that signaled the seasons. The rustling of the leaves in the trees on spring and summer nights and the raking up of those same leaves in October when the weather turned crisp. The cold stars through the bare branches. The taste of stolen peaches and apricots and the excitement of sneaking over a fence on summer nights to get them. Lovers throwing

pennies into the wishing well in the plaza on brilliant Sunday afternoons. The deep, deep blue of the sky. The call of the hills behind the town and the smell of the mesquite wood campfires. And further away how the stream ran cold and clear through the canyons and the spring water that came out of a crack in the solid rock of the canyon wall.

Ben thinks of the saying, *you can never go home again,* and knows that in his case it is truer than for most. He can never go home again because his home has vanished, like a dream.

A memory brings with it the tangy smell of exploded earth.

Ben stood guard on the road by the old hospital. He removed his hard hat and wiped away the sweat from his forehead and neck and looked up toward Heaven Hill. The houses were all gone but some of the trees still stood, green now in the spring.

The blast holes were loaded and fused in a circle around the top of the mountain. The crew foreman walked along the curve of the road and took up his position. He raised the red signal flag high and held it there for a moment. It fluttered on a soft breeze that brought with it the smell of roses. The foreman made the usual three circuits of figure eights and at the top of the completion of the third pass he brought the flag sharply straight down. Before the sound of the blast reached him, Ben saw the top of Heaven Hill rise up, hang suspended for a moment, and then settle slowly back down to the deafening detonation of forty thousand pounds of explosive. The sound rushed by and away. Then there was only silence and a hill of smoking rubble. Later it would seem to Ben that he'd heard voices in the rushing wind.

The images pile up too quickly to hold and study. Ben lets them flash by. He thinks of Helen and drifts slowly into sleep.

26

"Mr. Medina? Ben, are you all right?"

Ben opens his eyes. Cindy is standing at his bedroom door. There is a sharp pain in his back, and it is difficult to breathe. Cindy walks to the side of his bed and presses the red button on the wall. In a second or two the telephone rings. Ben hears Cindy speak into the telephone. "Please hurry, Mr. Medina is sick."

There is a jumble of images. Two men, dressed in white, appear. Ben feels the movement of being placed on a stretcher and the ride down the elevator. He is conscious of being transported in an ambulance. There is a very long, dark hallway with only a hint of a light at the end. A faint voice encourages him to move to the light. It is important. The hallway becomes very narrow and tight. It takes all of Ben's strength to crawl in the direction of the voice.

There are many people. Ben sees Helen and Sara and the twins and Kemper, but everything is dim and vague and unreal. Then, gradually, the people begin to dwindle until there are no more and then there are only brilliant dreams. Then the dreams are replaced by a soft gray world where Ben lives for a long time.

Ben hears the sound of voices. A man dressed in white is speaking to another man. They are talking about him. Ben concentrates on the other man. "Sal?"

Sal moves quickly to the side of the bed. "Ben. Yes, it's me."

"Where am I, Sal?"

"Here, in the Rose Garden."

Ben looks around. "This is not my apartment."

"No, you were at St. Agnes Hospital for a while. You had pneumonia. Now you are here in the assisted care side of the Rose Garden."

Ben turns his head to look out of the window of the second story down to the orchard. "I want to go back to my own apartment."

The doctor speaks. "Yes, Mr. Medina. After you are completely well, you may go back."

Ben looks at the doctor. He is very young. His voice sounds far away, and Ben is suspicious of him. He looks up at Sal's face. "Did I almost die?" The doctor answers, "It was critical for a while, touch and go." Ben offers his hand to Sal. Sal holds it in a firm handshake.

Ben closes his eyes again and when he opens them it is dark. A dim light shines at the bottom of the wall. He gets out of bed and walks down the hall. Soon, he is conscious of arms leading him back to his bed.

A man comes to visit him each day. He is a well-dressed man and Ben likes him. The man talks to him about a place called Orenville. Sometimes the man shows him a big book with pictures of a town and people. The man tells Ben stories about the people in the pictures. One time the man pointed out a house in a picture and told Ben that that was where he had lived. Ben did not believe the man and told him so. He became upset with the man. He told the man that he lived in Duluth and that he loved a pretty girl there and that he worked in the train station and at night he would write poems for her by candlelight. She would come for him to go to lunch at a small café down the street. There was a park across the way. She wore a pretty green coat and white gloves and she had snowflakes on her pretty brown hair. The man squeezed Ben's forearm and looked away.

There are times in the evening when a woman comes and sits in a chair against the wall close to his bed. Sometimes the woman is young and sometimes she is older. They speak to Ben about things he does not quite understand.

When Ben has no company, he likes to sit by the window and look down at the orchard. There is something about the way the sunlight dances along the graceful curve of the walkway through the trees that is very pleasing to him. He can look at that walkway for hours.

Today, Ben notices that the man who always comes to visit him has a tooth outlined in gold. Ben smiles at the man and motions him over to his chair. Ben whispers. "I went to China to look for gold." The man moves closer and places his hand on Ben's shoulder. Ben shakes his head. "I found a rose but there was no bread."

The man speaks. "There was no bread, Ben?"

Ben frowns. "No, it was lost. It was… lost… bread."

Ben drifts, then comes quickly back. He blinks his eyes and shakes his head. His eyes come into focus. "Sal?"

"Yes, Ben, yes. What is it?"

Ben's words come quickly. "I want to go back. I want to go back now. I want to see Heaven Hill as it was and walk along the roads and paths and alleys. I want to wave at all the people sitting on their porches as I walk by and I want supper waiting for me when I get home and I…." Ben loses his voice. There are tears in his eyes.

"Soon, Ben. Pretty soon we can go back."

Ben wonders about the man who comes and goes. He looks down at the orchard and sees the man walking away. The man stops and looks back toward Ben's window. Then the man starts walking slowly again, moving in and out of the sunlight until he disappears. Ben looks once again at the curve of the empty walkway as hints of memories flit about in his mind. The harder Ben tries to catch those memories, the further they drift away. Another memory flutters away and then returns to him of its own accord. It is there before him, bright and clear.…

27

A full moon rises over Heaven Hill and golden light spills out of the open doors of the Minero Dancehall. The sounds of the band tuning up float across the hills to Ben's front porch where he and China speak about saving money for the upcoming strike. They have put themselves on a tight budget and have stopped going to the movies and Ben now buys the cheapest beer available. He has discovered that the beer is not too bad if it is ice cold.

Ben removes two beers from the freezer and places another two back in and walks out to the porch. As he and China speak, they can see the cars beginning to line the road by the dancehall.

"Are you tired, Ben?"

"A little. Not too bad now."

More cars arrive at the dancehall. China laughs. "Boy, those people aren't afraid of a strike, are they?"

"No, they're fearless."

"Rita came over this morning and said that she and Sal were going to the dance."

Ben looks at China. "Sal and Rita are fearless also."

"Yes, there are some pretty fearless people around here."

The band plays snatches of a melody here and there. There is a pause in the music while Ben speaks casually about other matters and then the band begins to play in earnest.

They are silent as the music comes across to them. When the

song ends China speaks softly. "That sure is a pretty moon." She hums the tune of an old song.

Ben looks at the huge, bright moon rising in the sky. "Yes, China."

China stands up and walks to the end of the porch and then back again. She sits down and sighs.

Ben takes a long drink of the ice-cold beer. He speaks as though to himself. "If I only had a clean and pressed white shirt...."

China laughs. There is music in her laughter. "You do, you lucky guy."

At the beginning of the alley that leads to the road above the dancehall, Ben and China stop and kiss in the shadows of a tall cottonwood tree. China is wearing a new yellow dress, which she had made herself and which fits her perfectly. A young boy comes running down the alley. When he sees Ben and China he slows down to a walk and as he passes by, he says, *"Con permiso."*

China smiles at the boy and says, *"Pase, joven."*

They reach the top of the alley and walk onto the narrow road that climbs slightly and then drops down where the tightly packed houses along the way funnel the music towards them. There is applause and the noise of the crowd as the band finishes a corrido and begins a bolero. The deep, rich sounds of the saxophones swirl about in the soft spring night.

China sings the first line to the song. *"Amor, que pases tu vida ..."* Ben no longer feels tired. He looks over at China, beautiful in yellow.

As they reach the highest point of the road, China moves a few steps ahead of Ben and begins to sway to the rhythm of the music. For a moment she is framed by the moon, and the light shines on her hair and the sound of her laughter floats back to him. China holds out both hands. "Ben, let's walk in dancing...."

B en looks down at the orchard and tries to remember the rest of the words of the song. The shadows grow long as Ben holds on to his captive memory. He holds on until the sun moves low in the sky and falls behind the mountains and the trees lay in darkness.

Amor, que pases tu vida
Hasta el fin de tus dias
En saber sin olvido
Que siempre, y solo tu
Eras la gran luz de la mia

Love, may you go through your life
Until the end of your days
In knowing and not forgetting
That always, and you alone
Were the great light of mine.

28

I t was a long and untypical winter, cold and rainy with the occasional bright day thrown in between long stretches of overcast days. Then it passed and the good weather returned.

Sal looks out from Dr. Birch's office to the orchard where the rows of orange trees are in full bloom. He looks further along to the beginning of the winding pathway where at that moment three people come into view.

Dr. Birch is speaking.

"Younger people look at older people and see old people. They see the ravages of time from head to toe. Time and gravity. Everything says old. That those people were once young and strong and witty and pretty and quick and handsome does not cross their minds. All they see is the surface, and it looks old. They assume the inside is as well."

Sal laughs. "I hear that, Doc."

"That is the way of the world. People see what they see." Dr. Birch moves a folder on his desk towards him but does not open it. "This, however, is truly remarkable, Sal."

Dr. Birch pauses, seemingly looking for words. "And I don't think it was simply the new medication. Or, not entirely. It could be any combination of things. It's as though the illness, the pneumonia and near death, somehow swept aside the other symptoms or indicators. Like someone hit the reset button. I have heard of a few rare cases where this happens."

"Doc, I went to see him one day and he was fading fast. I thought this is it. But then a couple of days later there was a difference in his face but especially his eyes. Day by day he improved until he became the Ben not only of six months ago but even flashes of the Ben of years ago. When we walked back to his regular apartment, I could barely keep up with him. It's true he needed a nap afterwards but when he woke up, he said he was starving and if I wasn't ready for lunch, he was leaving without me."

Dr. Birch smiles at Sal. "Again, the body is an amazing thing."

"It may sound funny to you, Doc, but he told me that remembering the words of a song cured him. He had a long dream. A very long dream, he said. And the dream had everything in it. His whole life with details he had long forgotten and then at the end he heard a song. It was a song his wife used to sing but only the melody. Then the words came to him and remembering the words of that song cured him. He said he had been living in a kind of a fog for years and when the words fell into place he woke up and the fog was gone."

"Yes, well, who knows what new pathways the brain can devise? It could come back, or not, maybe tomorrow or ten years from now. For many decades we were told that brain cells did not regenerate. When they were gone, they were gone, they said. Now, new studies have discovered that they do."

Sal once again looks out of the windows of the office to the orchard. Ben and Helen and Sophie have arrived at a bench along the way. They are waiting for him. All their suitcases are packed and in the car. In an hour or so they will set out on a long road trip with no true itinerary or schedule. Just wherever the car points to. Maybe somewhere along the way they'll see an interesting high hill off the highway and walk to it and climb it. Maybe in a dancehall in some hidden away mountain town they will dance the night away. In some gaudy casino out in the middle of nowhere maybe they will shoot craps and laugh loudly and carry on while doing it. And just maybe they will cause such a disturbance that they will be asked to leave. What can they do to old people anyway?

And finally, maybe on their way back they will take a detour up the long winding road to Orenville and take their time and tell the ladies all the old stories about the old town and how it was back then.

Outside, Sal sees Ben pacing back and forth by the bench. He is animated and anxious to be off. He is smiling broadly and holds his arms out as though asking a question. Helen and Sophie are laughing.

Sal looks at the scene for a while. He thinks of the journey that brought them all to this place and time. "It's a beautiful day, Doc."

Dr. Birch follows Sal's gaze. In the morning sunlight of spring he sees three attractive and lively people. They are framed by green leaves, white blossoms, and blue sky.

"Yes, Sal. I think the world is always beautiful. What changes is how our eyes look at it."

The car has climbed up and over the mountains east of the Valley of the Sun. Now the long open road stretches out smooth and bright in the sunlight. It runs straight for many miles and then off in the distance it curves gently toward the northeast.

The new old Ben has taken over the conversation and is now telling the ladies stories about the Minero Dancehall and about some of the characters who used to hang out there. He is describing the building and how it was a large split-level affair because it sat on the incline of the hill, and how the lower level was the dancehall but also served as a theater and basketball court, and how the top level housed the bar and restaurant and pool hall, and how there was a bakery across the narrow rising road where the baker made the best bread and pastry of all time.

Sophie speaks up. "You know, that sounds like a place I've been to. Years ago, in New Mexico maybe. That town was also up high, and it seems to me that on one of the hills there was a dancehall something like the one you're describing. I can't for the moment remember the name of the town." She points in the direction of a mountain range far away on the horizon. "It's up that way. It might be in the mountains behind those mountains, or the ones behind those. Not sure. You climb high and go through a pretty forest and then through some lovely rolling hills. If you happen to approach it at night, it is quite a sight. You can't see it and then you go around the curve of a hill and there it is. Looking up at the twinkling lights of the town it looks very much like a jewel."

Ben and Sal can see it. The lights of a high town at night.

The car speeds along as the women laugh and talk in the back seat. The men smile and laugh also. The image of the town grows until it is all filled in.

The miles slip by. It is bright and clear and just past noon. Ben and Sal look out across the long miles of a wide valley to the high blue mountains far off where the thin line of the highway disappears for a while and then begins to rise.

It could be that somewhere up ahead they'll go around a curve and see a mountain town reminiscent of one now gone. A place with a hint, an air, an echo of another town in another time.

Maybe there will be a plaza there and a long climbing curve to reach it and then higher still to the roads leading up to the lights shining on the hills. And on one of those bright hills maybe there will be a dancehall where the music swirls out of the open doors into the night under the moon and stars up and down and all around.

Maybe it will be like that.

❖ ❖ ❖